HOOPS OF STEEL

JOHN FOLEY

HOOPS
OF STEEL

flux™
Woodbury, Minnesota

First Edition
First Printing, 2007

Book design by Steffani Chambers
Cover design by Ellen Dahl
Cover photograph © 2006 Deborah Davis/Photonica/Getty Images
Editing by Rhiannon Ross

Flux, an imprint of Llewellyn Publications

Library of Congress Cataloging-in-Publication Data
The Cataloging-in-Publication Data for *Hoops of Steel* is on file at the Library of Congress.
  ISBN-13: 978-0-7387-0981-9
  ISBN-10: 0-7387-0981-6

Flux
Llewellyn Publications
A Division of Llewellyn Worldwide, Ltd.
2143 Wooddale Drive, Dept. 0-7387-0981-6
Woodbury, MN 55125-2989, U.S.A.
www.fluxnow.com

Printed in the United States of America

I'd like to thank my former teaching colleague Stephen "Ole" Olson, who read an early draft of the novel and offered helpful suggestions. Alison Picard, my agent, also provided some fine tips and persistently submitted the manuscript to publishers. At Flux, Andrew Karre's insight helped improve several sections of the book dramatically, and Rhiannon Ross's eye for detail was a saving grace. Finally, I'm grateful for the inspiration provided by my students and colleagues, by my former coaches and teachers, and by the ballplayers of yesteryear from Holmdel and Keyport, New Jersey, and at Dominican High School in Whitefish Bay, Wisconsin.

For David Laughlin and his wonderful family.

ONE

*An ode to my youth, when the game of
basketball ran deepest and loudest and
clearest in my soul.*

—David Shields, *Heroes*

*T*he game is tied with twenty-five seconds left to
play. I'm on the wing, covered tightly by a tall girl.
Pushing her a little, trying to get free, and she's pushing
me right back, very competitive. I notice she has a pretty
face. I take my mind off that because it's crunch time.
And finally I get a step and Angelo flips the ball to me.
He's naked as usual, and I wonder why the girl is wearing a white uniform. I think of popping the jumper right

1

*then—I only need a few inches to get it off—and most
girls can't jump very well. Pelvic structure, I heard: good
for babies, bad for hops. Anyway, with just twelve seconds
left now I don't want to give her or her team a shot at
glory, I want it all for myself. So I wait, faking with the
ball, staying low. She crouches down too, looks me in the
eye, and smiles. I can't help but smile back and she flashes
a hand at the ball, almost slapping it loose. Sly temptress,
I think, and then drive to the baseline with a flying first
step, leaving my feet and . . .*

Crashing to the floor next to my bed.

"What the hell was that?" Granny calls from the
kitchen.

"Just getting up," I say lamely.

"Sounds like you're falling down, Jackson."

"No, it's all good."

"Breakfast is ready."

"Be right down."

Another hoop dream. Weird. I know from psychology
class last year that it's ripe with symbols, and that I can
learn from it if I think about it in the Jungian sense. The
symbols have some basis in reality, I remember. The girl
seemed familiar in a way, though I'm not sure exactly why.
And I do play basketball every day, lots of times in pickup
games with a guy named Angelo who likes to walk around
naked when he's not running the point.

At breakfast Granny says that I could be on time to
school for the first time this year. "That would show moti-

vation," she smiles over her coffee. My guidance counselor wrote on my report card last spring that I lack motivation, and Granny took that line and ran with it. Pretty much true, I have to admit. But mostly I lack motivation in my first period Algebra II class. I was not meant to divide negative integers at seven-thirty in the morning.

My favorite classes are Honors English and Journalism. In Journalism I'm learning how to be an objective reporter, which isn't easy. I'm the sports editor and so I have to write about some guys on the football team who I can't stand, and it's been tempting to hit 'em with a shot between the eyes. Something like, "Joe Fridley, a flaming asshole who naturally plays tight end, caught four passes Saturday to lead the Highlanders to victory."

God, I'd love to write an honest story.

I know I can't, though. Wouldn't be fair or objective. Mrs. Ford, the Journalism class teacher, is forever telling me and the other Journalism students to keep "I" out of our copy, to write in the third person, recording events like a camera. The exception is a column, so naturally everyone wants to write a column. But Mrs. Ford won't allow more than two columns per issue of the *Highland Beacon*.

Granny Dwyer begins cleaning up. I start to help, carrying over my dishes, and she shoos me away, telling me to get to school on time. So I grab my pack and head out the door.

I've known Granny since I was seven, and she hasn't changed a bit in ten years, at least not that I can tell.

Maybe her hair is a little whiter. She's seventy-four but doesn't look near that old. She laughs when I tell her she could pass for fifty-five.

She's not my real grandmother. Both of them died when I was young. The truth is she's just a nice neighbor lady who took me in after things went crazy last year. She treats me like I'm a relative, though, and I can talk to her about just about anything. Plus, she's a basketball nut.

The Dwyer house is just up the hill from the one where my family used to live, and I'd see her watching me out the back porch window while I shot around in the driveway. And when her real grandson, Gerry, invited me up the hill to play on his driveway when I was twelve, she'd pull up a lawn chair and be our lone spectator, clapping and laughing and offering advice, or just watching quietly.

Gerry is six years older than me, and what's so random is that he's now my English teacher at school. We're both cool with it—he didn't have to tell me not to act all buddy-buddy in class, like I was kissing butt for a better grade. Not that I care about grades anyway, but I just knew it would be better not to go around telling everybody that we were friends, and that he taught me how to shoot the jumper off the dribble long before he taught me to appreciate Shakespeare.

It bugs me sometimes that Gerry doesn't play much basketball anymore. He told me last year that he prefers golf now. Told me with a straight face. And he's the golf coach at school, not the basketball coach.

I ride my bike to school in September when the weather's nice. It's about three miles of easy pedaling, and I like to look at the tall trees and think about stuff. Plus, riding the bus sucks big time.

Morning is my favorite time of day. The air is sweet, the world new, the adults pumped on caffeine. I like the way the light hits the trees and fields. Not many cars use the back road I travel, so I don't really have to concentrate too much. I can just look around and sort of lose myself in the good feeling, the way I can when my shots start dropping through the hoop like guided missiles.

On this morning I think about the journal I have to keep for English class. I forgot to make my entry last night—read *Sports Illustrated* instead—so I remind myself to get it done first thing . . . I see a barn and hay stacks in a field, really pretty, and remember that my mom used to joke that Highland is a nice town, but unfortunately surrounded by New Jersey.

Back to the journal. Should I write in the first person, which seems natural, or third, which doesn't? "Jackson O'Connell had a wonderful day today, not including two additional zits on his chin." Sounds strange. Like those ballplayers talking about themselves in the third person. Whenever this is pointed out, most of them look blank—or worse, they start looking around for this third-person dude.

I once saw a football player asked about his constant third-person references in an interview. He smiled at the reporter and said, "God bless you." Like he thought "third person" was part of the Trinity—Father, Son, and Holy Linebacker.

A lot of jocks are pretty dumb. I know that's a cliché, but it's true. Maybe half are average or better. But it sure doesn't take a genius to hit a running back or a twenty-footer.

Mostly, I think my journal will be a diary of the basketball season. Our team at Highland isn't going to be spectacular, but I'm hoping to have a great year myself. It will also be fun to follow my friends' season at Shoreview High. Technically, Shoreview is Highland's arch-rival, but I'm not about to lose friends over that. Besides, it's fun to watch Shoreview play. They could go all the way to the state championship.

My goals are to average sixteen points a game and get a scholarship to a Division I college. Of course, I'd like to average twenty a game, but Gerry keeps urging me to be realistic, to face things honestly.

I suppose my journal will be mostly like a column, since I do have opinions and plan to include the word "I." But I'm going to be objective, too. Kind of look at it neutrally and report on the season, rather than spew out a bunch of opinions.

I gotta say, though, that my opinions about basketball are solid. If I don't know much else, I know the game. Maybe a few coaches around have read more books on the subject—maybe. I read every book in the school library my freshman year, every book in the public library my sophomore year.

Since then I've been hitting the bookstores and buying books when I have the money—which isn't often—and reading for hours. The clerks in the upscale bookstores with the soft chairs and classical music smile and say, "Still here?" And the clerks in the used bookstores tell me to get the hell off the floor and ask more often, and with an edge, "Still here?"

I also read all of Granny's library, and she has quite a few hoop books that are out of print. Autobiographies of Jerry West and Oscar Robertson, to name a couple. Granny has always been a fan, and I found out gradually, from Gerry, that she was one of the best women basketball players in the state when she was in high school.

One night over the summer, when I was going through her bookshelf, she brought me an old picture of herself posing with the ball. She acted a little strange—blushing and stuff. I could tell she was both proud and embarrassed to be revealing part of her past.

She looked great in the picture, lanky and pretty with her brown hair in a bun. I teased her about her uniform, which was a knee-length white skirt and white blouse. "Lawn bowling, anyone?"

"You laugh, but New Jersey was pretty liberal for its time," she said. "Most girls elsewhere weren't allowed to play organized basketball."

I asked if I could have a copy and she said of course. I really did like the picture. She had the ball close to her shoulder, eyes focused on some unseen hoop, and her mouth was determined but held a little hint of a smile. Sort of like Jennifer Love Hewitt shooting a trey.

Anyway, to return to the subject, I guess I've read a couple hundred books on basketball by now—instructional, biographies, histories, novels, you name it. I also practice at least three hours a day and watch games and commentaries on TV. So even though I'm still in high school, I'm really an authority on hoops.

So my take on our team this year is pretty well-informed. I think we'll be average, maybe a little better. We have two sophomores who look okay, seven juniors who are decent, and me, the outstanding senior forward. Another senior who played last year is a better baseball pitcher than basketball player, so he decided to focus on the slow sport in hopes of getting a scholarship himself. Leaving me alone at the top of the ladder.

I hope I have a year to remember.

TWO

Those friends thou hast, and their adoption tried, Grapple them unto thy soul with hoops of steel.

—Willy "Shake-n-Bake" Shakespeare,
Hamlet

I pop in to give Granny a hi and bye after school, grab my ball and head for the door. "Going to Danny's," I say.

"Okay, call if you're going to stay over." She waves at me from the couch, never taking her eyes off her game show.

It is exactly four miles from Granny's house in Highland to Danny's in Shoreview, and downhill, steeply or gradually, all the way. I start easy, waiting for the rhythm of the dribble to match my running rhythm. Sometimes synchronization comes after a hundred yards, sometimes after almost a half-mile, but it always comes.

I love running for the same reason I love basketball—I can disappear from real life into a dream world. Sometimes I go beyond dreams and enter a really peaceful kind of place. Sort of like where meditation is supposed to get you. A few years back Mom got into yoga and meditation as a way to cope with Dad, and she tried to get me hooked. So every day for about a month I'd do the strange stretches and then sit cross-legged on the floor, saying "om" and trying to box out stray thoughts—which is tougher than you'd think. I got bored, and decided that I needed to meditate on the move.

Running, I can reach that free and happy feeling more easily. Then the exercise becomes effortless and it feels like I can run all day.

A basketball meditation is even better. I can get into a zone shooting around by myself, and in my best one I made 118 straight free throws. The best ones, though, take place during games. Then every shot drops because I have absolute control of the world, and the players around me become sort of like partners in a dance that I lead.

Today, running to Shoreview, I just daydream, which is okay. I smile thinking about what Danny would say if I told him he was a dancer on the basketball court. We became friends just last spring, but we're real tight.

It's pure coincidence that Danny Larson is my best friend and also has the best driveway basketball court in the known universe. We met as competitors when we were freshmen. I burned him for eighteen points, which of course I never let him forget. We played against each other a couple of times as sophomores on the junior varsity team too, although he was improving and I only averaged about twelve points against him. Then I had to sit out my junior year with a broken shooting hand, but we ran into each other again last spring on a playground in Midland.

We were shooting at opposite ends of the court. We nodded to each other and checked out each other's jumpers, thinking about a game of one-on-one. Finally he walked over. "You're O'Connell from Highland," he said. "Sorry, I don't know your first name."

"Jackson," I said, shaking hands.

"Hey, Jackson, good to meet you. I'm Danny Larson."

"Yeah, I remember playing against you." Out of politeness I didn't add that he was a step slower than me.

"How's your team looking next year?" he asked.

"Okay, but not anywhere as good as yours. Bunch of juniors, couple of sophomores and me."

"Why didn't you play last year? I figured you moved."

"Nah, broke my shooting hand," I said, holding up my left. It was still pale and thin from the cast then, though getting stronger.

"How'd you do that?" he asked.

"A fight," I shrugged.

"That sucks," he said. "Probably hit the guy in the head, right?"

"More or less, his eye."

"That'll do it. Next time go for the gut. Keeps your hands unbroken and nobody expects it." He demonstrated with a couple of uppercut air jabs.

Danny plans to be a lawyer if a pro sports career doesn't pan out, and he is one of the few jocks I know who openly admits that it probably won't. The rest of us have the dream, even if we don't say so. You can feel the vibe.

Sometimes he'll say stuff like, "My backyard is probably as far as I'll ever get as a ballplayer." Everybody just stares at him, and he shrugs and laughs, cool with it.

Still, he's giving himself a chance at greatness, playing, besides basketball, tight end in football and catcher in baseball. As a basketball player, Danny's best attribute is his strength. He's a ferocious driver, almost impossible to stop once he gets a step and head of steam. He'll either get the hoop or a foul call. Occasionally he'll be called for a charge because the ref feels sorry for the poor idiot writhing on the floor, but most defenders aren't that brave.

I took a charge from him once our sophomore year and woke up in the locker room ten minutes later with an ice pack on my head and the trainer saying, "Jackson, how many fingers am I holding up?" Danny likes to tell that story whenever I recall burning him for a lot of points.

Danny's outside shot is a little streaky but solid enough to keep defenders honest, so he's really an effective scoring threat. He's fast—a couple of weeks ago I saw him catch a pass across the middle and break a sixty-yard touchdown—but not really quick. It takes him too long to get up to full speed. Otherwise, the only flaw in his game is a tendency to keep his head down on his hellbent drives to the bucket. As a result he doesn't see defenders come over to help or, more importantly, his wide-open teammates. They are forever trying to break him of the habit.

We played one-on-one that first day. I won three of five games, and could have won three straight but I let up a little out of politeness. I do that sometimes, to be nice or just keep things interesting. My dad used to say I didn't have the killer instinct.

After the games, Danny asked me if I wanted a soda. I told him I was broke.

"No problem, so am I."

"I'm not up for shoplifting."

"Not stealing, Jackson," he said. "Trust me. Follow me in your car."

"I don't have a car. "

He stared at me. "You must be the only guy in Highland without one. I thought it was pretty much required that you all had Corvettes."

"Not everyone in Highland is rich," I said. "I'm not."

"You're in the minority. How'd you get here?"

"Ran. It's only a couple miles."

"Well, come on, Jackson, hop in my Rusty Yellow Dog and let's blow this place."

So that's how our friendship began. A few miles of high speed driving and loud opinions later, he pulled up in front of a small store in Shoreview and beckoned me to follow him inside. Then he went over to the cooler, grabbed two sodas and handed me one. He popped his open right in front of the guy behind the counter and started drinking, making no move to pay. I hesitated opening mine, looking at the clerk. He was a guy in his fifties with a bald head. Then I noticed the resemblance.

"Dad," Danny said, "this is Jackson O'Connell from Highland."

"What, you bring the enemy into my place of work?" his father asked with a wink at me. Then he came over and shook hands. "Sure, I remember you, lefty with the quick step. Was wondering what happened to you last year."

"Broken hand," I said. "Had to sit out."

"How're you guys looking next year?"

"Not as good as Shoreview."

"That's because you don't have any niggers up there in Highland," he said. "You need some niggers to compete nowadays."

"Dad," Danny complained, noticing my discomfort. "Remember you promised Mom to stop using the N-word?"

"Okay, blacks, coons, whatever, you know what I mean."

Danny rolled his eyes and smiled at me. "African-American is the preferred reference," he said.

"You're sounding more like a lawyer every day," Mr. Larson said. "And it's not preferred by me. What a stupid name. Too long, and it gives the idea they're some special kind of Americans. You hear me calling myself an Anglo-American, for crissake?"

"We're gonna go shoot some hoops before you really get rolling, Dad."

Mr. Larson put his hand around Danny's shoulder. "Yeah, go have some fun," he said. They were close, talking to each other like friends, and it made me a little jealous.

Outside, we headed to the court in the Larson's driveway. It was my first glimpse of what was known as The High Court.

Soon after meeting Danny, I met Angelo and Thaddeus and the rest of the Shoreview players. At first they treated me with suspicion, like I was a spy, but eventually they realized that I just loved to play basketball. And so we all became friends.

I think it bothered Angelo a little that Danny and I became instant best buddies. They'd grown up together and everything. He didn't hold grudges, though, and we were cool.

Basketball brought us all together. Without the game they would have thought all guys from Highland were spoiled snobs. And Thaddeus Fly never would have set foot in the Larsons' neighborhood without the bond of basketball.

I'm still running, and my daydream ends when I look up and see Danny's house and The High Court coming into view. Four miles zip by in a good dream. And most of mine have been good lately.

THREE

How the team does affects my feelings about the game and myself; sometimes, I think, too much. I am obsessed with my work of team basketball . . . Some friends say I am function-ing in a world that bears little resemblance to reality. At times I feel as if I am an artist in the wrong medium.

—Bill Bradley, *Life on the Run*

Gerry Dwyer's class is on the second floor, near the back, and is avoided by teachers while attracting students like a hip new club. And in a way, it is. He purchased some used furniture over the summer and set up comfortable chairs and couches in place of the all-in-one, plastic seat, fake-wood desks that were not meant for people over six feet—or really people in general.

The walls are decorated with prints of famous paintings, mostly by the Impressionists, and all that color gives the room a vibrant and friendly feel. He also placed large-print quotations from writers all around. Shakespeare: "To thine own self be true." Robert Frost: "Always fall in with what you're asked to accept. Take what is given and make it over your way." Aesop: "No act of kindness, however small, is ever wasted." And a favorite of mine from an Irish writer named Kendall Hailey: "Happiness is like everything else," she wrote. "The more experience you have, the better you get at it." And dozens more reflecting his literary taste.

Some students mistake Gerry's room as a sign of weakness and try to take advantage. He doesn't let them. Sleeping on the couch, for example, means you have to stand for the rest of the period. He always gives you a choice, though: stand or go to the office. Put a quarter in the cuss bucket if you slip, or go to the office. I've never seen him have to send anyone out. Maybe because he handles students with more care than most teachers. Like the ballplayer he was, he always keeps his cool no matter how angry or inappropriate the student might act. And he listens.

Gerry's only real pet peeve is cell phones. He told me when we were shooting around one time that he thinks it's really rude to pull out a phone when someone is trying to teach you. By the way, I'm about the only student at Highland High without a cell phone or a car. But Granny lets me borrow her car all the time, and she'd get me a phone if I asked. She's already done so much for me, though, that

I'd feel bad asking. Plus, Danny and my sister are the only people I call on a regular basis.

Anyway, Gerry enjoys catching "cellphonics," as he calls cellphone addicts. "The hunt begins when I spot the inattentive prey," he explained. "Nearly always the young beast has his or her head down and therefore does not spot me as I slyly move toward the lair. I keep the other beasts distracted with rhythmic patter, and when I'm close enough, I pounce."

I've seen him in action. He really does pounce. It's funny and the student is too shocked to argue with the detention penalty.

Gerry's also a tough grader. He'll flunk you if you don't do the work. He told me privately, though, that he doesn't go strictly by what the computer average indicates. For example, he'll bump a high C to a B for a student who worked really hard, or one who started slow but made a comeback. "Don't tell anyone," he winked at me when I dropped by as he was finishing up grades last year, when he was a rookie teacher. "I want to keep my rep as a tough grader. It's about the only thing Edwards and I agree on."

I could understand why Gerry rubbed Principal Edwards the wrong way. He doesn't look the part of the typical conservative Highland teacher. He wore jeans last year until they banned them for the staff, and open collared shirts until a tie was required. Still, his tie is never knotted tight, and his khakis, while clean, seem to have a permanent case of wrinkles.

One time when he was over for dinner at Granny's, he joked that he was personally responsible for the new teacher's dress code at Highland. "They didn't need one until I showed up," he laughed.

Gerry has a small apartment down at the beach, but he drops by Granny's for dinner once a week, to see how we're doing. Last time he got to talking about how he doesn't really have too many friends on the staff, and how some of the older teachers flat-out despise him.

"I don't socialize much with them. Most of them are older, and they hang around the lounge and gossip, complain about students, teachers, administrators. I was getting depressed over lunch. And when I had the gall to disagree with some of them on a few issues, boy, it got ugly. So I eat in my room now, and I'm sure they've since added me to their complaint list."

"You're a fine teacher, Gerry, it runs in the family," Granny said. "Don't you pay those bitter teachers any mind."

"Believe me, Granny, I don't. They're just putting in time until the weekend—and retirement—and could care less whether students learn anything about their subject or life."

This afternoon, as we file in, Gerry is giving us high-fives. Every class has at least one "Dwyer Moment," as we've come to label his quirky ideas. For example, a few weeks ago, on a beautiful autumn day, he felt so inspired he scaled his desk and sang "Climb Every Mountain" from

The Sound of Music. Just as his fine tenor reached a crescendo, Principal Edwards walked in. We all applauded. Edwards didn't join in the clapping, he just stood there with an annoyed expression. Then he cleared his throat and asked if he could speak with Gerry privately in the hall for a moment.

Some of us worry about Gerry being a rebel without a future.

"Today being a Friday," Gerry announces, "I thought we'd play a little game. First write in your journals while I take attendance, and then I'll explain. The journal topic today is touch. Not shooting touch, O'Connell," he says with a wink at me, "but human touch, like we just had at the door. Some questions you might consider: Why is touch important? How can you establish touch without being offensive?"

"Take a shower!" shouts Marvin Renker, a linebacker in the back row.

"Okay, Marvin, I'll buy that," Gerry smiles. "Now write about it."

We set pens to paper. I don't write the same things in my English journal as I do in my Journalism journal. Gerry usually provides a topic, so it's more like a commentary than a journal. So now I write about touch, and how the flirty sweep of a girl's hand across my shoulders—pretty rare, but it's happened—can make my day. Gerry, meanwhile, finishes attendance and walks over to the computers in the back of the room and fiddles for a few minutes. Then he sets up two chairs side by side, facing a garbage can on top of a table ten feet away.

"What's going on, Gerry?" asks Kelly Armstead.

"It's Mr. Dwyer, Kelly," Gerry says.

"Well if you're going to be that way, it's Ms. Armstead, Mr. Dwyer."

"Fine. Finish your journal, Ms. Armstead. I'll explain in a minute."

Kelly looks over at me, smiling and shaking her head. We're kind of friends, sharing mutual interests in basketball and journalism. Everything about Kelly is long. She's six feet tall, has dark brown hair that falls halfway down her back, long arms, long legs, long nose, long jaw. Kelly's long on smarts, too—she's a lock for valedictorian, spends first and second period taking a college math class at a community college, and has a full academic scholarship to Princeton. She took the SAT as a sophomore and scored close to perfect.

Sometimes, if we're talking basketball or writing or everyday stuff, I can actually communicate fairly well with Kelly. When she gets riled up about politics or economics, I need a translator. Usually I don't even know why she's mad, so I just nod my head until she realizes I'm not capable of debating the topic and moves on to someone more informed.

"Okay, finish your journals and listen up," Gerry says. "I know I'll have to explain this twice, but I'd like to not have to explain it a half-dozen times, so please listen. I'm going to divide you into two teams. The first representative from each team will start at the computers. I've written the first sentence of a story. You have to add three sentences to the story. The idea is to keep the story going and provide someplace for your teammates to take it. The caveats for the story are: no profanity, no sex, no violence, no drugs or alcohol."

"What a bummer story, dude!"

"Hey, Mr. D, is shooting an AK-47 violent if, like, no one gets killed?"

Gerry shakes his head. "Let's leave out guns, Trevor, okay? Use your imagination, don't regurgitate what you've seen on TV . . . Now, after you write your sentences, you move to the dictionaries. You need to look up a word with four or more syllables. It can't be a proper noun—someone's name, for instance, or a place like Mississippi."

"Do we have to use the dictionaries?" Renker asks.

"No, Marvin, not if you can think of a long word without it, although you might want to check the spelling."

"Cool," Renker says with a mischievous smile.

"Okay. After you have your word, you write it in a sentence on the board, trying to use it precisely as possible. And make the sentence as clean as possible, paying attention to grammar, spelling, all the conventions."

"Is it a sentence from the story?"

"No, the sentence on the board has nothing to do with the sentences you write on the computer."

"How come?"

"Because it's my game and that's the way I designed it. Now, after you finish your sentence on the board, the one containing the four-syllable word, you have to shoot this ball into the basket." The ball he pulls out is larger than a softball, smaller than a basketball, and made of newspaper and Scotch tape. The "basket" resembles a common Highland High garbage can. "The last person on the team to go will be the rebounder. You shoot until you make the shot, then you tag a teammate and the process is repeated until everyone has gone. Questions?"

"You stay up at night thinking of this stuff, don't you, Mr. D?"

"All night every night, the D is for dedication. Now let's talk scoring. The first team to finish gets twenty points, the second team ten points. The team with the best story gets ten points. And the team with the best sentences gets ten points. Do the math—you can finish first and still lose. Understand? The idea is to be fast *and* good."

"We should play guys against girls," says Ivory Lewis, "because the guys in here are fast but definitely not good." There is whooping from the girls and howling denials from the guys. Ivory is a knockout with a bad reputation. Comments like that are typical for her and don't help her image. Not that she cares. She's smart, can pass for twenty-four, works part-time as a model, and has basically left high school behind.

"Ivory," Gerry says after getting everyone settled down. "Let's keep our remarks appropriate for the classroom, okay? In fact, I'm going to charge you a quarter for that."

"I didn't cuss!"

"Innuendo," Gerry says, "which by the way, is a four-syllable word. Now pay up or head down to the office."

She pulls a quarter from her too-tight jeans and sways over to the cuss bucket and plops in the money, knowing every eye is riveted to her. The walk involves a lot more innuendo than what she said, but Gerry lets it pass. He explains the rules of the game again, and promises to help anyone who struggles during the contest.

"What do we get if we win?"

"My everlasting admiration and two extra-credit points on your essays due next week, which you can work on while waiting for your turn," Gerry says.

The game begins. I'm the designated rebounder for my team, and Gerry stops the game briefly to amend the rules when I use my chest as a backboard. "Just toss the ball back to the shooter, rebounders," he says. "No bank shots off the human backboard allowed, O'Connell." He always calls me by my last name in class, maybe just to put a little formality between us, let me know we're not shooting hoops in the driveway.

After a few players from each team complete the rounds, everyone catches on and the game proceeds smoothly. Until it's Renker's turn. When he gets to the blackboard, he looks around to be sure he has an audience, then writes, "Edwards is a motherfucker."

"Marvin!" Gerry snaps. "You know the rules about profanity! Erase that!"

"I thought that was just verbally, not for the game," Marvin says, erasing while everyone continues to laugh.

"No, I specifically mentioned that no profanity could be used in the game."

"For the computer part, yeah," Renker says. "You didn't say anything about the sentences on the board."

Technically, this is true. I can see Gerry debating whether to send Renker out or let him stay because of the loophole. "Marvin, I think I made it clear I don't want to see profanity in your writing, either. Now use another word or you're going to have to personally explain to the principal why you've written such an offensive sentence about him."

"How do you know I'm talking about that Edwards?" Renker asks, drawing another laugh. Before Gerry can reprimand him again, he says, "No sweat, Mr. D," and turns back to the blackboard, pondering. And pondering. The game is close, so his teammates get on his case, urging him to look for a word in the dictionary. This makes him more stubborn. His feet are planted and he's obviously not going to move until he can catch a big word swimming around inside his massive skull.

"Marvin, Marvin," Gerry says sadly. "If that's the only four-syllable word you know, you've got to get some new CDs."

FOUR

> *But the intention of play was far different in Naismith's mind than it is in the minds of today's players, coaches and enthusiastic spectators. Winning a contest was an afterthought, much subordinated to more important altruistic notions of camaraderie, healthful competition and physical exercise, and good clean fun for all participants.*
>
> —Peter C. Bjarkman,
> *The Biographical History of Basketball*

Like I was saying, The High Court is located in Danny Larson's yard. The court is at the far end of an extra-wide driveway. Actually, the driveway is standard width as it comes off the street, but expands once inside the wooden fence. There is a semicircle of tar that clearly marks the boundary of the court. Scuff marks from a thousand sneakers show where the driveway becomes sacred ground.

The hoop is located on a garage that Mr. Larson built with two purposes in mind: providing a sound structure for a rim and housing his cars, in that order. The concrete building is located off to the right as you pull in the driveway, leaving plenty of room to shoot from the left corner. Most driveway basketball courts have maybe ten feet of room in the corners. We can go out to twenty on The High Court.

Just inside the wooden fence is a towering oak. The tree has a massive branch that points in a direct line toward the basket, like an arm ready to throw down the dunk of dunks. Mr. Larson clamped a spotlight on the branch, and this enables us to play ball (and annoy his neighbors) deep into the night.

Between the two garage doors is a wall about two feet wide and eight feet high, painted Celtics green. This is one of our favorite features at The High Court. What we do is run toward the wall holding a basketball, place a foot about four feet up, spring skyward and dunk. Most of us just need one step, but of course Thaddeus doesn't need the help of a wall to throw the ball down, and Angelo needs three steps. He's only five-two, and one of the amazing sights at the court is watching him climb the wall with his quick feet to slam the ball home.

The rim at The High Court is reinforced and exactly ten feet above the driveway. Mr. Larson sealcoats the driveway and replaces the rim annually. He paints the wood backboard and garage twice a year. Replaces the bulb in the spotlight every four months. And strings up a new nylon net monthly.

I think it's cool that he tends his son's basketball court and lets his lawn go to hell.

What lawn there is, anyway. There isn't much. Once it became clear that The High Court was the center of neighborhood activity, and would be used on a more or less daily basis, Mr. Larson took action. To his neighbors' horror, he paved over most of his yard. So we can play our standard three-on-three games and still have room for half a dozen cars in the driveway. Those waiting for the next game—and some summer nights it might be three teams—usually lounge on top of the car hoods. "Hoods on hoods," Mr. Larson calls it, especially if there are several black players waiting.

Not many come by anymore. The problem started last summer, when, to the embarrassment of me and the other guys, Mr. Larson decided to explain the difference between black people and niggers. We all had our heads down, checking each other's reactions out of the corners of our eyes, but none of us had the guts to say anything.

Except Thaddeus.

Thaddeus Fly is the king of The High Court. And of all courts in the area. We call him Fly for short, Thaddeus formally, and no one ever, ever calls him Thad. Danny told me a guy from Bayonne called him Thad during a game, trying to psyche him out, and Thaddeus burned him for forty points.

I first became acquainted with Thaddeus Fly my freshman year, when I threw him my best fake. I use it in the low post every game for a few scores. What I do is get the ball on the blocks with my back to the basket. Then I pivot and fake a fallaway jumper. The move is really effective, naturally, after I've hit a couple of fallaway jumpers. Anyway, I really put a sincere head, ball, and shoulder fake on whoever is covering me, and four out of five guys jump to block the shot. Then I dribble once around them on the baseline and shoot an easy layup.

I started the game with a baseline fallaway, so it wasn't surprising that Thaddeus fell for my fake a few plays later. What *was* surprising was that I was staring at his size twelve Converse All Stars. Sure, I was crouched down after the pivot, but his feet were still higher off the ground than I would have thought possible without the help of a trampoline.

I overcame my shock, took a dribble, and hit the layup about the same time he touched down from outer space.

As we ran up the court, he said, "Nice move, man." Then he hit seven straight shots on me. I was playing him tight, and was almost as quick as him, but he simply leaped over me to score inside and wasn't bothered at all by my hand in his face outside. On two of his shots I was helping out on defense when this midget point guard—Angelo—penetrated to the lane. I cut him off and he kicked the ball over to Thaddeus on the wing for mid-range jumpers. We called time, and Coach Green told me not to leave Thaddeus. "If he takes a dump, I want you there holding the toilet paper, O'Connell!"

I got the message and covered Thaddeus tight all over the court. I kept him from getting the ball a few times, but then they started having football players set screens on me. The only time I "stopped" him after that was when one of the football guys got carried away and knocked me down in front of the ref.

One thing I noticed that game was that Thaddeus was never rushed or frustrated. Even his quick moves appeared slower than they were because they were so smooth. When we had the ball, I ran hard, trying to get him tired, but he just played his superior game with an ease that pissed me off. He never gave me any room. When I forced a jumper, he didn't just get a hand on it, he knocked it into the third row. And his ability to recover was unbelievable. After that first move, I never completely faked him out. I thought I did a couple of times, and was laughing my way in for layups, but he recovered in time to block my shots.

I'd never played against anyone with that much talent before, and it woke me up. The guy was just great.

All I managed the rest of the game were a couple of garbage buckets and two long jumpers when I got good picks and his teammates didn't switch in time.

Soon after that game I decided that I'd have to be a role-type player. Like most guys, I wanted to be a star, but Thaddeus showed me I wasn't qualified. It wasn't too upsetting, because I found that if I played hard, set picks, hit jumpers, and focused on teamwork, I was really a solid player. My new game was effective against just about everyone, and helped me fit in with anyone.

I gotta say, most players don't learn this lesson. They try to do too much. Like, it's the rare guy who has a consistent inside and outside game. And most players are more concerned with looking cool than playing well. Some of these guys crack me up. You burn them with jumpers and smart passes, shut them down on defense, help your team to a big lead, and then they get one lousy dunk and they shout and point and act like they are the second coming of LeBron James.

Even Thaddeus gets tired chasing me around sometimes and I can score some points on him. It's a matter of pride that I was on each of the only three teams that have ever beaten a Thaddeus-led team on The High Court. We all know Thaddeus will be playing in the NBA in a few years, so beating him in a pickup game is something special. Each of the wins, I was at my absolute best, and Thaddeus was a little off his usual amazing game. I'm proud just the same.

Anyway, as the best player on The High Court, and probably the best in ten states, it was natural that Thaddeus should confront Mr. Larson that day.

"Mr. L," he interrupted in his deep voice. "I don't feel comfortable around people who use the word nigger, and neither do my friends. And we'd appreciate it if you didn't say that no more."

For a few seconds, Mr. Larson just stared at him, like he couldn't believe what he was hearing. "You gotta be kidding me," he said finally. "You people call each other nigger all the time, but the word is off limits to me, on my own property?"

"It's like a family thing," Thaddeus explained. "We can call each other nigger and it's all in the family. You ain't part of the family. No offense, sir, that's the way it is."

"Not for me," Mr. Larson said, but before he could continue the debate Ronnie Seals, one of the black starters for Shoreview, decided to have his say. "You wouldn't like us calling you a white racist motherfucker, now would you?" Ronnie asked.

Mr. Larson's face and head turned crimson and he stepped toward Ronnie, finger wagging and mouth shooting the ugly word like bullets. Danny, who would have sided with his father against his friends and teammates if it came to that, settled for stepping between them and pulling his dad away. Mr. Larson was seriously pissed, and was still trying to get at Ronnie, so Danny finally lifted him in a bear hug and carried him to the house. It would have been funny if everyone wasn't so upset and angry.

No black guys came by The High Court for several weeks, despite Danny's apologies and his promises that his father would be cool. Then Thaddeus showed up out of the blue one day in early September. He didn't say anything, but it was understood that Danny's apology was accepted. I wondered if Thaddeus came back because he wanted to be Danny's friend or because he wanted to have harmonious race relations on a team that could go all the way to the state title. Maybe it was a bit of both.

It was understood too that Mr. Larson was sorry that he'd embarrassed Danny, and maybe a little sorry he'd insulted the black guests on The High Court. He made a point of inviting Thaddeus in for dinner and not using the N-word or starting any racial crap. He was so careful it made him kind of subdued and not his usual funny self. Anyway, Mrs. Larson handled most of the dinner table conversation, asking Thaddeus friendly questions, and never approaching the minefield of race.

I wondered if it would have been better just to air everything out in the open. But that isn't the way of ball-players, the neighborhood, or the Larson family. Communication in these groups is a pretty low-key business following a fight, consisting of small gestures of reconciliation. I've seen brotherhood in a bounce pass, forgiveness in a free ticket, peace in a pepperoni pizza.

And I've seen Thaddeus Fly create bonds of friendship and tolerance almost as well as he creates shots on the court.

FIVE

*The Sunday morning game was the high holy
tradition among the males of the neighborhood.
At Hale School Courts, Sunday meant shaking
your sorry self out of bed to slam and jam those
Saturday night cobwebs away, Jack . . . What
they knew was ball. Ball dished out the stories
they spent all week in clubs and bars
around town. Ball raised up princes and
threw down kings.*

—Rand Richards Cooper,
Straight in Your Face

On the first Sunday in October, I perform my weekly
duty and escort Granny to early Mass. This is the
only thing she really requires me to do, other than clean
up after myself and let her know where I am, which I'd
do anyway. Church is another story. I wouldn't go if it
were up to me. While Granny clutches her rosary and
hangs on every word of the priest, my mind wanders all
over the map, my eyes over all the girls.

After church I make scrambled eggs, bacon, and wheat toast for brunch. Then Granny and I clean up the kitchen and living room. I'm having the Shoreview guys over in the afternoon to watch the Giants and Bears play, and I want the place to look nice. First we're going to play a few pickup games at the Ross School Courts. The school is technically in Highland, but the neighborhood borders Shoreview. At school the Ross area is known as "the ghetto," even though it's actually a regular middle-class neighborhood.

It's about eleven when Granny drops me off at the courts. She's heading over to a friend's house in Rumson to play cards and socialize, and she'll be back after dinner. That should give me plenty of time to get the place clean again.

A pickup game is already in progress, and the Shoreview boys are waiting on the sideline, ready to stomp the winning team. I say hello to everyone. "Just made it, Jax," Danny says. "I thought we were going to have to pick our fifth from the losers."

"Had to get Granny some breakfast. You guys still coming over for the game after?"

They all nod and say yeah, definitely, except Ronnie Seals. He says he can't make it. Though he no longer considers me an enemy spy, we haven't become friends. He's not tight with Thaddeus, Danny, or Angelo, either, though they're all seniors and have played ball together since they were shooting underhand. Ronnie likes to keep some distance, hang with other guys or just be by himself. The only time it becomes an issue is when he carries his solitary attitude onto the court and starts shooting too much.

Actually, Ronnie should never shoot the ball, because he has the ugliest shot I've ever seen. Even saying what he fires at the hoop is a shot is being generous. It's more a throw that starts from behind his head and never leaves his hand exactly the same way twice. Most of his shots are knuckle-balls or have a slightly forward spin. Everyone winces when he winds up to fire, and it's a good day for him when he makes twenty percent of his shots. Danny says their coach, a legend named Richard Gowans, has worked on changing Ronnie's shot for years, without any luck.

If Ronnie plays within his limitations—rebound-ing, playing tight defense, setting picks, and passing the ball—and the rest of us play our usual games, we are all but unbeatable as a unit. After Thaddeus and I played together a few times during Sunday runs last summer, and he heard about my home situation, he pitched Danny and Gowans on having me transfer to Shoreview. Danny was all for having me as a roommate in his basement apart-ment, since I stay over once or twice a week anyway. But Gowans said no, he didn't like the idea of a Highland guy transferring onto the team for the sole purpose of help-ing them win a state championship. He wanted to win with "real Shoreview players," Danny explained, the four seniors and half-dozen so-so underclassmen. We were both disappointed, but I understood the decision. I'm not a real

Shoreview player. I also don't feel much like a real Highland player.

The game ends and we walk onto the court to warm up. The winning team that we'll play has three players from Monmouth College and two former high school heroes. I've seen them around. They aren't in college and work part-time jobs while they figure out what to do with themselves beyond basketball. The game is everything to them and they play with real heart. Even with hangovers, this team would beat us if we didn't have Thaddeus, though we might give them a decent run.

The game begins and Thaddeus immediately drives by his man and dunks lefthanded. His man lays off the next time down and Thaddeus buries a jumper. The third time Thaddeus drives again, the guy covering me tries to help out, and Thaddeus dishes to me for an open jumper from the corner, which I hit. And so it goes until our lead is five. Then Thaddeus takes himself out of the game a bit, lets Angelo and Danny get some points, and doesn't even scold Ronnie when he throws up an airball from twenty feet.

We play three games, win them all easily, and the Sunday morning run is over. Resting on the grass with our backs against the school wall, sipping orange juice and water, we are rendered speechless when Ivory Lewis strolls over and sits down facing us. She's smiling, ankles crossed, breasts barely constrained by a halter top.

"Jackson, how's it going?" she says, patting my leg. I hadn't realized she knew of my existence, much less my name. I take a couple of seconds to recover. "Uh, hi," I say with stunning intelligence.

"Aren't you going to introduce me to your friends?"

"Uh, yeah. This is Danny, Thaddeus, Ronnie, and Angelo," I say. "Guys, this is Ivory Lewis, we go to school together."

They mumble hellos, trying not to stare. She fixes her cat eyes on Thaddeus. "Are you THE Thaddeus? Thaddeus Fly, the basketball star?"

"One and the same," he says, and we laugh. They shake hands for a very long time. "Pleasure to make your acquaintance, Ivory."

"Well, now that we've met, let's be friends, not acquaintances."

"Sure, just a figure of speech."

"I heard you have some great moves, Thaddeus," she says with a flirty smile. "Can you show me one?"

"Yeah, Fly," Danny says with a smirk. "Show her your moves."

Thaddeus glares at him, a little annoyed, then snorts a little laugh and shakes his head as he walks with Ivory over to the hoop. She manages to throw a hip into him a couple of times on the way.

"Oh, young-a-love," Angelo sighs. "I think I'm-a-gonna cry."

"Shouldn't be messing with that," Ronnie mumbles.

Ivory giggles every time Thaddeus shows her some move. The session ends and they exchange cell phone numbers. He places it in the pocket of his sweats. They do the long handshake thing again, and she places her other hand on his shoulder and gives a squeeze.

We leave Ross Courts a little after noon. I ride with Danny, and Angelo rides with Thaddeus. I'm glad they're coming over. I invite them fairly often and Danny regularly, because I feel I owe him for all the hospitality the Larsons have shown me. They rarely take me up on the offer, although Danny will often step inside to say hello to Granny and gulp a quick soda after dropping me off. While I often run to Shoreview, Danny always gives me a ride back to Highland. He does it because he's a good friend, but he likes to claim he's checking out his future neighborhood.

The neighborhood doesn't impress the others as much. "No pizza joint, no bowling alley, no movie theater," Angelo said the other time he was over. "Why would anyone want to live here?"

Another reason for the rare visits is that Gerry's court, while nice, can't compete with The High Court. Plus, Highland is a rich town overall. I was a little uncomfortable the last time they were over and Thaddeus asked me where I used to live. We walked to the backyard and I pointed down the hill. As they took in the acre lot and sprawling Colonial, Danny whistled, Thaddeus shook his head, and Angelo noted that it must have cost some serious bank. And I felt a crazy need to explain that the house really wasn't that great and I didn't miss living there.

Everyone seems more comfortable today. I shoot around with Thaddeus while Danny and Angelo are showering inside, and we're playing a casual game of HORSE. This is the only game in which I can actually beat Thaddeus. We're closely matched as shooters.

He makes a couple of jokes about the neighbors calling the police because a black guy is in the neighborhood, and we laugh ourselves silly when a cop rolls past on cue.

"You're dropping the property values by the minute," I joke. "I'll bet the whole neighborhood is checking you out with binoculars and telescopes."

"Long as that's the case, I might as well show 'em something." From deep in the right corner, he dribbles toward the basket, gathering speed. He flips the ball behind his back with his right hand. It sails over his left shoulder as he leaves the ground. His right hand recovers the ball a foot in front of the rim—and a foot above it—and he slams it home backwards. As usual, he makes it look easy, like a reverse one-hand dunk off a running behind-the-back pass to himself is something he's been doing all his life.

"I'll concede an O on that shot," I say, not wanting to praise him directly. Ballplayers just don't do that, even if they are impressed. I wait for the hoop to stop vibrating before attempting my next shot. Thaddeus winks.

He beats me by a letter, I promise revenge, and we head inside for showers and the football game.

Granny made up some pizzas for us, and I put them in the oven at the end of the first quarter. Angelo and Danny are sipping beers they brought along. Neither Thaddeus nor I drink. Like him, I want to be at my best as a player all the time, and that's tough when you're under the influence or battling a hangover, like the college players. We could smell the alcohol sweating out of their pores on the court . . . I don't want to end up like my father, either.

At halftime, with the Giants ahead 14-3, Angelo walks out of the kitchen holding a dripping slice of pizza. He's also naked.

Angelo's not gay—he'll fight anyone who says he is—but he has a strange urge to walk around naked sometimes.

"Giants are looking good," he says around a mouthful of pizza. "Almost as good as the Italian stud Angelo D'Angellini, yeah, baby." He spreads some sauce around himself.

"What the hell you doing?" Thaddeus demands.

"That's right, Fly, you've never seen Angelo's act, have you?" Danny asks.

"Not this one."

"It's getting old," I mention. The first time I saw Angelo's show was last spring at Danny's house, when his folks were gone for a few days. We'd finished a driveway game and were watching the NBA playoffs when Angelo suddenly emerged naked from the bathroom and walked around the Larsons' house like it was no big deal. I waited for Danny to say something, but he just continued to watch the game. Finally I said, "Hey, Angelo, if your clothes are smelly or something, I have an extra pair of sweats you could borrow."

Angelo doesn't seem to mind that we either ignore him or tease him about his strange habit. He takes a seat on the couch next to Thaddeus, who trips over the coffee table trying to get away.

"Yeah, laugh at *me*," Fly says standing a good ten feet from Angelo. "Is this what white guys do to chill? Sit around, drink beer, get naked, and spread pizza sauce on your dicks?"

"Hey, you stereotyping us, Thaddeus?" Danny asks with a grin. "Just because one short, demented Italian likes to do this . . ."

"I'm big enough where it counts, yeah, baby," Angelo says.

". . . doesn't mean all of us do."

"My bad," Thaddeus says.

"Seriously, Angelo," I say, "please put your clothes on. This isn't my house, it's Granny Dwyer's house, and if she comes home unexpectedly . . ."

"What? She'd call the cops? Folks in Highland don't get naked, Jax?"

"Not in the living room during the Giants game."

"I just wanted to cool off."

He heads back to the kitchen and the phone rings. He picks it up and starts talking in a relaxed conversational manner, and I realize, with a sudden sick feeling, that he's talking to my little sister. I run into the kitchen and grab the phone away from him.

"Hey, Shannon."

"Hi, Jackson. I was just talking to your friend Angelo. He sounds nice."

"Yeah, real nice. Can you hold on a sec?"

"Sure."

I cover the receiver. "What the hell are you doing talking to my sister when you're naked?"

"She doesn't know I'm naked."

"Hey, it's the principle, Angelo! Put your clothes on. Jesus!"

"Okay, okay."

I talk to Shannon for ten minutes. She's doing well in school, enjoying herself, and sounds happier than I've heard her for a long time. After I hang up, a sudden surge of joy hits me—a feeling of harmony, like everything is well and as it should be. Seeing that it's Sunday, I count my blessings: My sister is happy; Granny is saintly; the morning hoop run was perfect, the pizza delicious; my friends are laughing; the Giants are winning; and Angelo D'Angellini is once again wearing his clothes.

All is right with the world.

SIX

*Kicking the ball is a violation when it is a
positive act; accidentally striking the ball
with the foot or leg is not a violation.*

—*Official Rules of Basketball*

Today in Journalism I write a football preview and plan to interview the girls' cross-country star during lunch. I'm sweating just thinking about it. Joan Farrell is a junior who is pretty in an undernourished kind of way.

She's one of those people who are constantly smiling. She has more varieties of smiles than Starbucks has coffee. A few I've seen from a safe distance include the slight corner smile, the closed little laugh smile, and the perfect teeth and dimples biggie.

My concern at the moment is the five zits on my face and neck. I have this hopeful idea that all my zits will magically disappear when I turn eighteen in May, a fabulous present from God and Clearasil. Who knows?

Ever since my face and neck became a minefield in eighth grade, I haven't been able to confidently talk to girls. Not that I was Don Juan before that or anything. The problem then was shyness. And just as the shyness started to fade a little, whammo, my skin blossomed. Then last year I found a good reason to disappear, and my skin gave me added incentive.

Anyway, I now have sort of a professional excuse to talk to a nice-looking girl. I must do it, I must. I'm fully psyched and will not, under any circumstances, run away from the interview and find the nearest basketball court to calm myself. I swear I won't.

Mrs. Ford, who has a few kids herself in addition to the hundred and forty or so she teaches, picks up my anxiety. "I thought you were past getting nervous about interviews, Jackson," she says, and I realize I was mouthing questions, like a dress rehearsal.

"Oh, I'm okay," I say. "No sweat, I can handle it."

Mrs. Ford smiles. "Who is she?"

"She?"

"Sí, she."

"Um, Joan Farrell, the cross-country star."

"Don't run away, she could catch you," she smiles. "Good luck."

"Uh, thanks."

At this point Kelly Armstead, pounding away at an editorial, echoes Mrs. Ford. "Yeah, good luck, Jackson."

She doesn't even look at me as she says this, and I'm surprised at the sarcastic tone. A stray idea forms, but it can't be right. Kelly wouldn't be interested in me, she's too far out of my league in the brain department, the one person who makes me feel like a dumb jock. And I've never thought of her as a potential girlfriend. She's not really hot looking or anything, not in the usual sense. Her face is too long, although she does have pretty brown eyes and a nice smile.

Maybe I was imagining it. I look over at her again. She's still absorbed in her writing, and obviously doesn't want to explain, so I shrug and head for the door. Brilliant people and girls are tough to figure out.

I stick a notebook in the back pocket of my jeans, like a real reporter, and head to the commons. This is where lunch is served at Highland High. There are a few unstated rules about the commons that you violate at your own risk. First, underclassmen and upperclassmen cannot sit at the same table unless they are related, on the same team or club, or dating. And you just don't sit down at a table at which you're not a regular, unless you want some major stares and whispers and putdowns.

I used to have some friends I could sit with. We went our separate ways. Now they wouldn't consider speaking to me, though we were once pretty tight, laughed at the same jokes, played on the same teams. That's the way it goes.

In the cafeteria I spot Joan Farrell sitting at a table with a couple of cheerleaders and jock friends. Half a dozen girls, and I have to walk over there . . . Maybe I can just skip the interview and make up the whole thing. She looks like a decent person, maybe she wouldn't complain if I made her look witty and wonderful.

Coward, you're a coward, Jackson. Go now!

I walk to the table. The girls are talking loudly and hands and hair are flying all over the place. When I'm ten feet away, all conversation and action stop like someone pulled a plug. They stare at me, and the stares are, on the whole, unfriendly. Why am I pissing off females today? Or is this leftover from last year's coldness?

"Hey, Joan," I say. "Congrats on your win the other day."

"Thanks."

"Mind if I ask you a few questions for the *Beacon*?"

She smiles and shrugs. "Okay."

Conversations resume and the death stares are not as intense, to my relief. I reach for my notebook. My hand brings it around from my back pocket, very cool, except that I'm nervous and my palms are sweating. The notebook slips out of my hand and flies across the table, striking one of Joan's friends smack in the forehead.

"Hey, you jerk!"

"Geez, I'm sorry! You okay?"

She glares at me. She sneers at me. She shakes her head at me. This fearsome threesome doesn't seem to have the desired effect, so she grabs my notebook off the table and fires it back at me, aiming for a retaliatory head shot. I reach up instinctively and manage to grab it out of the air, like a pitcher snaring a line drive when he's really just using his mitt to protect his nose.

This makes her even more angry. So she picks up her cheeseburger and flings it at me. Her aim is off this time. The burger sails over my left shoulder and strikes a stoner in the back of the head with a slapping sound. He looks around, pissed, and one of his buddies screams, *"Food fight!"*

The commons erupt in a hail of all the major food groups.

SEVEN

*The one thing he hated in the game and
which offended his own sense of purity was
the player who faked a foul, who exaggerated
the impact of a collision by his own theatrics.
At the basketball camp where he taught tough
physical basketball, he obstinately refused to
teach how to fake fouls. It was, he thought,
phony and it was on the increase in
the league.*

—David Halberstam on Dave Cowens,
The Breaks of the Game

The principal's office at Highland is located above the lockers and facing the surrounding commons. I'm sitting in a chair facing the principal's desk, and have a nice view overlooking the tables in the lunch area, although it's obscured slightly by a smear of mustard.

Mr. Edwards enters holding a cup of coffee. As usual he's wearing a red power tie and white shirt. I don't think I could ever work a job that requires me to wear a tie. Most guys feel that way when they're in high school, I guess. Then they decide to wear one so they can get a good job, so they can get a nice car, so they can get a hot babe, and the next thing you know they have a couple of kids and a mortgage and they wear a tie so much it starts to look sort of *normal* on them.

I feel the same way about lawns. I never want to take a tie or a lawn seriously, like my old man did. Especially a lawn. You take a lawn seriously and the rest of your life becomes a joke.

"Well, Mr. O'Connell, you've had a busy morning," Mr. Edwards begins as he sits down. "Let's see, it seems you've been assaulting a young lady and starting a food fight in which three students were injured by flying debris."

"I'm sorry," I say. "I hope they're okay." I have a hard time believing anyone got hurt, because I had a good view on ground zero.

"The nature of the injuries is not the issue," Edwards replies. "The issue is your behavior."

"I didn't hurt anyone or start the food fight. It was all an accident."

"An accident?"

"Yes, sir. I was interviewing Joan Farrell for the newspaper . . ."

"And you slapped your notebook across the face of Rhonda Scott, who was sitting next to her. I must say that's an unusual journalistic technique. Is that what Mrs. Ford is teaching you?"

"No, and that's not what happened. My notebook slipped out of my hand and hit her by accident. Then she started throwing food, not me."

"That's not what she claims."

"Well, what I just told you is the truth."

"Did you throw any food, Mr. O'Connell?"

"Uh, yeah, I did. But only after I was hit by a taco."

"What did you throw?"

"Couple of cheeseburgers. Nothing serious."

"Nothing serious? Three students were injured, and this is nothing serious?"

"I know I didn't hurt anyone with cheeseburgers."

"That's what you *admit* you threw, what you *claim* you threw," he says. He's a thin guy, a runner, and he's pointing a bony finger at me. "But you might have thrown an object that could have seriously injured someone—a lunch tray, for example—and simply neglected to mention that, isn't that true?"

"No, that's not true. I would have told you if I did anything like that. I'm telling you the truth."

"Hmm, the truth again. We seem to have various versions of the truth, as usual."

"Why would I admit throwing food at all if I was going to lie to you about other stuff?" I ask. "Wouldn't it make more sense to just lie about everything?"

"I don't know, Mr. O'Connell, I'm not as familiar with the criminal mind as you seem to be."

"I didn't lie," I say, feeling my face grow hot, "and I didn't do anything criminal."

"Rhonda Scott says you came over to the table at which she was seated and started throwing your notebook and food. That scenario seems valid," he gestures with his hand toward the commons, "given the condition of the lunch area."

I'm thinking about mentioning witnesses, then realize the primary ones are Rhonda Scott's friends. Talk about unreliable. So I just repeat that she's not telling the truth.

Mr. Edwards studies me. With his eyes narrowed, he looks like a vulture. He taps his pen lightly against his lips. "How are things going for you, Jackson?" he asks at last.

"Just fine."

"No repercussions after the incident last year?"

My face is burning again and I feel like running out the door. "No," I say.

"Hmm. And you are now living with—do I have this correct—Mr. Dwyer's mother?"

"No, his grandmother. His mother and father retired down to Florida, so there was lots of room in the house. They were our neighbors. Gerry doesn't live at home anymore, so I help take care of his grandmother. It's a good deal for everyone."

"And I see," he says, looking down his nose through his reading glasses, "that Mr. Dwyer is your Honors English teacher? I didn't know that until now, and never would have approved it. Conflict of interest, you see."

"Teaching me English is a conflict of interest?"

"Don't get smart with me, Mr. O'Connell," he says, whipping off his glasses. "It's a conflict because as . . . as close acquaintances, he might be inclined to give you a better grade than you deserve."

"We're not acquaintances, we're friends," I say. "And Gerry—Mr. Dwyer—would never do that."

"Gerry, hmm?"

I sit and wait while he replaces his glasses and stares at me again. He's like a fisherman and I'm like a mackerel, and he's either going to club me or throw me back into the "school." From what I heard, Edwards likes to have something on students, especially screwups and troublemakers, to keep them in line. I'm guessing I'm now on his screwup list. Maybe the troublemaker list, too.

"I don't like what I'm seeing in your file, Mr. O'Connell," he says. "Problems at home, issues in chemistry class a few weeks ago, low grades in several subjects. Another reason I wouldn't have allowed you in Honors English is your low cumulative grade-point."

"I have straight As in English, and I'm doing very well this quarter."

"Yes, an achievement that I'm sure has nothing to do with your admitted friendship with the teacher." He sighs and shakes his head. "Be that as it may, I'm concerned that you may not be among our graduates next June, given these other problems."

For a second this threat feels familiar, and then I realize he's like some guys I've played against. Intimidating guys. They push you around, and if you lose your cool and fight, you get ejected and maybe hurt, and they win. So you just play like the guy's not there, holding your ground but not taking it personally.

"No comment, hmm?"

"No need, sir. You're just wrong."

He sputters and runs his hand along his forehead, which is reddening. "I don't appreciate defiance from students, Mr. O'Connell, especially ones who hope to play varsity athletics."

I figured he'd threaten my basketball season next. I'm getting better at reading people and figuring out their motivation. It's sort of like analyzing a character in a novel. They all want something.

"Didn't mean to be defiant, sir. I'm just telling the truth."

"No, you're telling me your version of events, and these differ from mine and others and, I might add, reality."

"I disagree, sir."

"Stop calling me sir, this isn't a military institution."

"Okay, Mr. Edwards."

"That's better. Not that your politeness isn't appreciated, Jackson, I'm just trying to get to the bottom of this."

"I understand, Mr. Edwards. I know you're hearing a lot of different stories. But I've been here four years and other than that little chemistry mishap, this is the only time I've ever been in your office."

"That 'little chemistry mishap,' as you put it, shut down the school for almost a half-hour."

"I take responsibility for that, but really, I think everyone overreacted—sort of like my experiment." He doesn't smile and I immediately regret the attempt at humor. "Even Ms. Ossinger said it was no big deal, just harmless gas."

"Which another staff member mistook for smoke and pulled the fire alarm. And he was correct to do so. We have to take such precautions when students are in our care. In this litigious age—sorry, you probably don't know what that means . . ."

"Means people sue a lot."

"Yes, very good, I see Mr. Dwyer is at least keeping your vocabulary sharp. In any case, people sue a lot, as you say, and so we, as educators, must be very, very careful. Hmm?"

"Yeah, I understand."

"This is my concern today as well. While no one was seriously injured in the food fight, they could have been."

"Someone could have been."

"Yes, that's my point."

"No, I mean we do a little grammar lesson in Mr. Dwyer's class every day, and we went over how pronouns must agree with their antecedents. 'No one' is singular. 'They' is plural. Agreement can be tricky." We sit there for a moment. I can't believe I just corrected the principal's grammar, and neither can he. I didn't mean to, it just popped out. I'm guessing he's really going to club me now.

He stares at me for a long time. "Yes, Mr. O'Connell, agreement can indeed by tricky. However, I didn't bring you in here to discuss the language. Because of your relatively good record, I'm going to make an exception and not suspend you for this incident."

He pauses, like he wants me to kiss the hem of his suit and yell, "I am not worthy!" I settle for saying thanks.

"I want no more incidents of this kind or the consequences for you will be severe. Am I clear?"

"Yes, Mr. Edwards."

"Then you are dismissed, Jackson."

As I reach the door, he says, "We're expecting great things from you on the basketball team this year."

"So am I."

EIGHT

*When you're the top dog, everybody
wants to put you in the pound.*

—Charles Barkley,
The Book of Basketball Wisdom

Usually I refer to the other guys who will play on Highland's varsity basketball team as the Junior Jagoffs. The only one who is real and not full of himself is Steve "Stoner" Dirkson. He's a proud product of the Ross "ghetto" and jokes that his family's house is smaller than most garages in Highland. A lot of the houses here are flat-out mansions.

To give Stoner his due, he's an excellent point guard. Problem with him is that he's way too fond of the weed, which explains his nickname. I hate covering him in pickup games because he breathes that shit all over me. In fact, that's his best move, a hot breath of weed in your face and a step-back jumper. He has an excellent shot, especially from the angles, where he shoots pretty line drives off the board from twenty feet. Great ballhandler and passer, too, although he tends to throw the fancy one rather than the easy one. And Stoner doesn't play much defense, considering that task beneath him.

Stoner is the only guy I talk to at all. The Jagoffs don't like him much, either, because he hangs out with other stoners and doesn't fit into their preppy jock category. I've tried to talk to the others, be friendly and stuff, and even saved a few of their sorry butts when I was a sophomore and they were getting hazed. But they started putting me down behind my back and ignoring me when I'd say hello before pickup games. They'd look at me like I farted.

So I gave up all attempts at communication. I'm going to do my best to be a good teammate and all, but that's a two-way street. Anyway, the rest of the probable starters are Jagoffs Chipper Michaels, Dale Browner, and Ted Sorenson. They are conceited, mean, spoiled rich boys who think they own the world. That's an objective comment, by the way. I'm sure a poll of the student body would back me up.

Like them, I used to be a little spoiled. I'm not any-more. I really don't think I was ever mean, at least not that I can recall offhand. And my volcanic acne has kept me humble.

The Junior Jagoffs are in fine form this week. After school when I'm leaving the locker room, I hear Michaels say, "Why is O'Connell coming out? Nobody wants him on the team." He says it to Browner, but I can tell it's timed for my ears. Makes me feel bad, and it takes two hours of shooting at Granny's before I feel okay again. I always feel better after shooting around.

I like shooting by myself or with my Shoreview bud-dies. That's the thing about basketball, you can play by yourself or with others. Sex is like that too, I guess, although I'm positive it's better with a girl, whereas basket-ball is great either way.

Anyway, while I'm shooting around, the question I keep asking myself is, Who cares what Chipper Michaels thinks?

And the depressing answer is that I do. If I'm honest, I do care. Despite my attitude with Mr. Edwards, I care way too much what everybody thinks about me, and they know it. The reason I stood up for myself pretty well in Edwards' office was that I was mad he was falsely accus-ing me and bringing up the stuff from last year. But who wants to go around mad all the time? Especially when you're doing something fun like playing basketball?

Gerry recognized my tendency to try to please people and earn their approval. Said he had the same problem in high school, and that it stemmed from trying to please our fathers, who were overly critical.

"The eldest-son syndrome," he said one evening last spring when we were shooting hoops in his driveway, which by then was *our* driveway. "They want us to be better than they were, to succeed where they failed, so they push us. And usually they push too hard, especially in athletics. It's a contradiction: they want to be proud and take some credit for our success, but they don't want to admit that we often fall short because we've inherited their inferior genetic traits!"

"Well," I noted, "Danny Larson is an eldest son, and his father doesn't push him. He's supportive and all that, but he doesn't tell him to go practice more or buddy up to the coach or anything."

"No, the syndrome doesn't always apply. Some men see through it. They can step back and look at their kid objectively. I like to think I'd be that way if I ever had a son. I'd also introduce him to less popular sports like swimming, cycling, golf, and tennis that he can enjoy for a lifetime, and make it clear that academics are more important than any sport. But I'd try not to push too hard in academics, either. We're slaves to our inferior mental genes, too."

"You don't have inferior mental genes, Gerry."

"Thanks. Neither do you, Jackson."

"I have a two-point-two grade-point average."

"Have you ever really applied yourself in school?"

"Well, no."

"Hence the low grade-point. If you focused more on school work you'd be right up there at the top."

"Not in math," I said. "I suck in math."

"I'm missing the good math gene myself," he said. "Straight Cs all through high school."

"How did you get through math in college?"

"That's the nice thing about college. Unlike high school, you get to choose most of your classes. I managed to avoid the math building at Rutgers for all but one class, in which I earned my usual gentleman's C."

I fed him for perimeter jumpers while I thought it over. I'd never really thought about college, just life beyond that in the NBA.

"There is another aspect of genes you should be aware of," Gerry said. "Look, I'm not judging your father, we all have our faults. But he's an alcoholic."

"Yeah, he is."

"So is my dad."

"Really?"

"Yes. He's dry now, recovering. But I can relate some to what you've been through, Jackson. You never know who is going to walk into the house at night. Will he be the happy drunk or the mean drunk?"

I nodded. "My old man was usually the mean drunk, the last few years."

"So to play it safe, you tried to please him. As I did my father. And that carries over to other people as well, people who will take advantage of you. You don't have to please anyone but yourself, Jackson."

"Sounds kind of selfish."

"It's not. You don't help other people by trying to please them. You help them by telling them the truth, providing an example of a noble and examined life, and maybe guiding them a bit, if they want guidance."

"Wow. I never thought of that."

"I didn't think about it much myself when I was your age. But you grow up, you change."

I smiled at him. "You take up golf and lose your jumper."

"Lose my jumper? I think not. Game of HORSE right now, pal."

And so we matched shots and mild insults while the sun lazed toward the horizon.

NINE

Eventually, everybody loses, ages, changes.
And small triumphs—a great play, a moment
of true sportsmanship—count, even though
you may not win the game.

—Phil Jackson, *Sacred Hoops*

Already the first quarter of my senior year is history. Report cards are handed out today, and must be returned in the next couple of days with a parent's or guardian's signature. My grades are, uh, interesting. As I glance over my report card after school in the gym, Tim Rolands walks up and sits next to me in the bleachers. Tim is the head janitor at the school, a short guy with huge forearms and a boxer's compact build.

"What's the news?" he asks. I hand him the report card, and he looks it over, then shakes his graying head and chuckles. "Well, pretty obvious what your strong and weak points are anyway. Maybe you're smart enough to know what you're dumb at."

"I have a pretty good idea of the dumb. Math. Science. Anything mechanical. Anything requiring a foreign tongue."

"There you go. It's like that guy who tells the doctor, 'It hurts when I do this.' So the doctor tells him, 'Don't do that.'"

Tim was head janitor over at the elementary school I attended, then was moved to the middle school I attended, and finally the high school. So it's sort of like we're going through school together, even though he'll be here long after I'm gone, unless his lottery ticket comes through. That's a running joke with us. I'll ask how it's going when I see him and he'll say, "The big ticket hasn't hit for me yet."

A couple of years ago I'd be embarrassed when Tim talked to me in front of friends. They would tease me about being buddies with a "loser janitor," although they were careful to make their remarks after Tim was out of earshot. I'd never heard about him hitting a kid—he'd have been fired for that—but he carries himself in a proud way that warns the putdown predators that this is not a man to mess with.

Of course they continue to talk behind his back. Anyone who doesn't measure up to the economic standards of doctors, lawyers and successful businesspeople is considered a loser in Highland. The exact cutoff point is unclear, but a rich girl in my history class last year declared, "If you're not making a phone number, you're not really making it."

I mentioned that comment to Tim one day, and he said, "Hell, I'm happy to be making a zip code." My area code monthly allowance is really pathetic by Highland standards, not to mention my lack of personal wheels and a cell phone. But most of my Shoreview friends don't get much money from their parents, either. They work their butts off at jobs after school and over the summer, and I understand the resentment they feel toward Highland people.

As I got to know Tim better, I learned that he was aware of what some students said about him. "They're sheltered and spoiled kids who don't know anything about the world, so why should I care what they think?" he said, which I thought was a cool attitude.

In a way, we started out as friendly enemies. Tim's job was to clean the school and keep it safe. My job was to get into the gym after school on rainy days to shoot around. All I needed was an open window in a bathroom or a teacher walking out late, and I'd be inside with my ball, shooting in the half-light. Tim learned to look for me on unseasonable days and listen for the echo of a distant dribble.

I'd never argue with him when caught. I'd just wave and leave the building as directed. Then one rainy Friday in the spring of my sophomore year, Tim caught me in the gym but didn't send me out. Instead, he called me over and gave me a soda.

"I used to sneak into the weight room when I was in school," he confessed. "I loved to pump iron. Still do, though not as much. Pushing a broom all day, I get enough of a workout. I'm doing my job kicking you out, Jackson. There's no supervision in here, so it's a liability thing for the school district if you get hurt."

"No way I'm going to get hurt shooting around," I said.

"That's how I figure it. And you practice enough and make it to the NBA, maybe you remember who let you shoot around and give me a percentage of your signing bonus. I'm not greedy or nothing, say ten percent."

"You got it, Tim."

"Deal then. I'll leave the men's room window open for you on snotty days. But only you. You bring anybody else inside, deal's off. I don't trust nobody else." We shook on it, and I've been training in the gym on rainy days ever since. Tim will hear the ball and come in and watch a bit, sometimes even feed me for shots, and we'll have a soda on his break.

Today, Tim stands, stretches his back, and gets ready to go back to work. "Seriously, though, Jackson," he says before going. "You should work harder in school. You don't wanna end up like me, pushing a broom for a living." I don't know what to say, and Tim walks off with a wave.

My problem as a student is boredom. Once in a while, though, the subject in a typically boring class will coincide with something that interests me—statistics, for instance, since I've been calculating hoop stats since I was nine. And when that happens I'll shock the teacher and do well. Always fun to shatter expectations.

Nothing shocking this quarter. Here's a rundown of my classes so far.

First period is Algebra II, which I just don't understand or have a desire to learn. The problem is compounded by it being the first class of the day, so I'm always late. This drives Mr. Warner crazy—or at least it used to. He'd get all wound up and give me detention, and I'd try not to laugh. Detention for me means sitting in the library with the other violators and reading a basketball book. Not exactly punishment in the classic sense.

At Gerry's recommendation, I went to see Mr. Warner after school one afternoon. He was surprised to see me. "Mr. Warner," I began, following Gerry's advice, "I respect you as a teacher, and I'm sorry I'm not a better student."

"Okay," he said warily. "You could be a better student if you showed up on time, did the homework, and stopped daydreaming in class. What's your point?"

"My point is, I don't see higher mathematics or even medium mathematics in my future. I can add, subtract, divide, multiply, calculate fractions and some algebraic equations, and figure any basketball statistic you want to know. Other than that, I just don't care much about math."

"You should care, Jackson, if you want to go to college. You're going to have to take calculus as a freshman almost anywhere you go."

"I don't have any college plans, Mr. Warner, at least not yet. So, I figure I'll cross that bridge when I come to it."

He thought that over. "Second semester there's a statistics class being offered. Maybe you should think about that to fulfill the rest of your math requirements, given your interest in sports stats. Algebra builds on previous knowledge, you see, and you're going to get further behind in here."

"Okay, I'll switch at the semester," I said, and thanked him.

"No problem," he grinned. "I always try to stay on good terms with my larger students." We've gotten along better since that little chat, and he's appreciated that I've tried to be more prompt and less dreamy.

Second period is gym. An easy A for me, always, so it balances out the D in Algebra. I like most sports. Right now we're playing touch football, and I'm playing quarterback and receiver. Does my ego good that some of the varsity football players have said I should have come out for the team. Anyway, I take my morning shower after gym class and emerge fully awake afterward. Most of the others just throw on some pit spray and spend the rest of the day smelly with dried sweat. I show up for third period clean.

Third period is French II—I call it French Duh—which I just don't have an ear for. And that motivation problem crops up again. I've never opened the textbook. Most of the time I'm involved in a spitball fight with a junior auto mechanic named Finks. We probably haven't said ten words to each other, but I consider him a friend in an odd way. He just grinned and started chucking spitballs at me the first day of class, a spontaneous reaction. And of course I returned fire. Kid has a great arm, and I need another shower after French.

The teacher, Mrs. Katz, hardly ever turns around to face the room, which is just as well, since the walls are so dense with the dried splatter of spitballs it looks like papier-mâché day in art class. Most of the students steer clear of Finks and me. We have the back row to ourselves, he on one side, me on the other. We tear ammo out of our notebooks, chew until moist, then fire at will. Our little war is fought to the rhythms of unaccented and poorly enunciated French. Needless to say, this is another D class for me.

Fourth period is Journalism. Fun, challenging, and another A. Mrs. Ford digs my work and I'm learning a lot. The interviewing part was tough, but I've found that my curiosity about people generally overcomes my shyness about asking semi-strangers a bunch of questions.

I'd get an A in lunch if it were a class. I'm following the lunch lady's advice about avoiding milk for the sake of my skin. I usually gulp down my food while walking to the library, where I spend the rest of the time reading a basketball book. I'm not exactly welcome in the commons since last year.

Fifth period is Chemistry. Mixing stuff together is okay, but I like a more random approach than the teacher, Ms. Ossinger, prefers. This explains why I've been responsible for two minor explosions and one building evacuation. "Jackson," she's always telling me, "it's not like trying out a recipe in the kitchen." We get along okay. She respects that I don't resent a D and beg for mercy at grade time, like some of the other unmotivated folks.

Finally, sixth period is English. I do have an ear for Shakespeare and poetry, love stories of any sort, and I'm learning to love writing. And while Gerry is my friend, I do the work and earn my A.

So that's the rundown: three As and three Ds, giving me a grade-point average of two-point-five. More than enough to be eligible for basketball, which is all I care about, really.

Later, I hand the report card over to Granny for inspection and signature. "Jackson," she says after studying it a while, "I've never seen a report card like this."

"It's an original."

"Certainly is. I hope no one thinks Gerry is giving you good grades just because you and he are friends."

"Mr. Edwards mentioned something about that a couple of weeks ago, after that food fight I accidentally started. And I think he might put me in another English class second semester. I hope not. Gerry is a great teacher. Believe me, Granny, he made me earn that A."

"I'm sure he did." She looks up at me and smiles. "Where do I sign?"

TEN

I went through the day numb. I sat through
my classes. I had to wait until after school to
go home. That's when I hurried to my house
and I closed the door of my room and
I cried so hard. It was all I wanted—
to play on that team.

—Michael Jordan
on being cut from the varsity team,
in Bob Greene's *Hang Time*

I feel like a rabbit that's been run over by a bulldozer. Roadkill in the rearview mirror.

At the team meeting held in Coach Moran's social studies room today, a couple of weeks before the first practice, he begins by ignoring me. Bad sign. But wait, it gets worse. Next he dubs this a "stepping-stone year," meaning he knows that teams with a bunch of seniors are going to spank us.

"You guys will be the top dogs next year," he says, then glances at me. "Most of you, anyway. This year we're going to learn. You step up a few levels this year, then summit next year, we'll make the state tournament."

I hope they'll be hit by an avalanche, as long as we're using mountain-climbing analogies.

"Now from what I've seen, we have some talent, but talent isn't enough, boys. You gotta have heart and be willing to learn. Make the regional tournament, that's the goal this year. Regionals this year, state next. All the way next year!"

There is some mild rah-rah from the Junior Jagoffs. I can't believe he's giving a "Let's get 'em next year" speech before the season has even started.

After the meeting Coach Moran calls me aside. He sits with a diet soda on his desk and his hands laced behind his fat neck, leaning back in his chair. He has a walrus mustache that lifts on the right side on those rare occasions when he smiles. He's a weightlifter and his huge arms are his pride. All year round he wears short sleeve shirts and tank tops while coaching to show off his guns. He was a football player and fair power forward in high school, from what I heard, and he continued to play football in college. Now he's an assistant football coach and head basketball coach, though I don't think he knows all that much about hoops. His strong point is that he doesn't take any crap. Not from students, athletes, parents, administrators, anyone. His weak point is everything else.

"Now O'Connell," he begins, "you're a senior this year . . . what's your first name again?"

"Jackson," I say.

"Right, Jackson. I'm going to be frank with you, Jackson. This is a rebuilding year."

"Yes, sir?"

"Now see, the problem is that you're a senior. The only senior. And you didn't play last year . . ."

"I was hurt."

He stares at me. "Don't interrupt me, O'Connell. Whatever the excuse, you didn't play last year. You did and it'd be different, maybe. Now I got a situation where I'm building for next year and have seven juniors and two sophomores who need experience. And frankly, that's my priority."

I feel tears burning behind my eyes, but fight them hard. He's not going to use me? I'm the best player in the school!

"Seen you play pickup ball," he adds, standing and walking around. To my relief he doesn't seem to realize I'm on the edge of losing it. "You're pretty solid. Quick first step, fine jumper, good passer, okay defender and rebounder. Another team, you could be a starter. But you got two things working against you here . . . make that three. You didn't play last year, so you got no varsity experience. You're a lone senior. And let's face it, you're no blue chipper."

Suddenly I'm pissed off. I want to Sprewell him right there in the office.

"I think I'm good enough to get a scholarship, Coach."

"Not likely, Jackson. You have good straight-ahead quickness but just so-so lateral, and the one flaw in your game is ballhandling skills. Put that all together and there's no way you can play guard in college. And at six-three that's what you'd be, a guard. You're a natural forward, but what Division I college needs a six-three forward?"

"I might grow."

"Yeah, and I might run for president."

"My father grew a couple inches in college."

"Good for him. But see, Jackson, I'm not going to throw away the future so a senior who *might* grow *might* get a scholarship. Sorry, that's the way it is."

"So you don't want me to come out?" The question has been sitting there for a few minutes. I needed to work up the guts to ask it.

"I didn't say that. I can't use you in the way I know you're thinking about. You want to be a star, like every kid and my grandmother. But what I want matters, and I want you to fill a role."

"What role?"

"You play your ass off in practice against these guys, it'll help 'em improve. Cover 'em tight on defense, make 'em work, that's the main thing. On offense, I want these guys shooting the ball. Of course if you're wide open, you let fly. Otherwise I want you being a frontcourt playmaker, you have the passing skills for that. I need to get the juniors the feel of shooting the ball in game situations."

I wait and he waits. It would be a Mexican standoff except he's got all the guns.

"Would I start?"

"Nope. I see you coming off the bench, sixth or seventh man. Get you maybe ten minutes a game, to spell Chipper mostly."

I almost gag. Bob "Chipper" Michaels isn't half the player I am. And I'd be his sub. I want to throw a ball in his face as hard as I can. I mean, what is this crap? I'm the senior! I'm supposed to get the star treatment, not some Junior Jagoff with his nose up the coach's butt!

"That's the deal, O'Connell. Take it or leave it."

"Can I think about it?"

He looks at me with a sneer, mumbles something, then nods. "Yeah, O'Connell, you can think about it, study it this way and that, right up to the first day of practice. That practice is at two o'clock the Friday after Turkey Day. You show up, I'll know we have a deal. You're not there, I'll know we don't. Now excuse me, I have some work to do."

I'm in a daze as I ride my bike home. It's cold and the wind earlier in the day has blown a fair amount of smog out to sea, so I can actually see some stars, maybe more than I've ever seen before around here, though they can't compare to the stars I've seen at basketball camps up in the Poconos. Looking at the stars always makes me feel better.

I think about quitting. I can just play pickup ball in Shoreview, have fun with my boys, graduate, and then maybe walk on to a college team. Or maybe join the Marines. I heard they play some good ball in the service, and I could use my twenty-twenty vision to become a sniper and take out Coach Moran from a thousand yards.

How could he do this to me? And how can I be so cool in the principal's office one day and come close to losing it with a coach a few days later?

I'm too shocked to be really miserable yet. So I just pedal along and stare at the woods and the shadows. I didn't think things could get worse than they did last year. Thought I was making progress, but now I'm right back at rock bottom.

Nearing Granny's, I realize I just can't face her right now. She'll sense something is wrong, and when she starts questioning me, I know I'll lose it. Usually I shoot around when I'm down, but that would just remind me of my situation with Coach Moran. No, I have a better idea.

First I stop at the store on the corner and buy a bag of German pretzels and a Coke. Then I head to the tree house, going around the back of the neighborhood so Granny won't see me. I push my bike quickly up the driveway of our old house—looks like the new owners aren't home—and lean it against the base of the big oak.

The tree house looms overhead. I helped build it, along with Gerry and a lot of the other neighborhood kids. The steps we built are looking worse for wear and a few are missing, but I'm a good tree climber, and in a moment I'm sitting inside our old fortress, where we used to overnight a dozen times during the summer.

I make myself comfortable, hands laced behind my head, still watching the stars. And thinking about all that's gone wrong in the last year. The big fight, bitter breakup and divorce, family scattering, breaking my hand, losing the season. Even my zits got worse.

I think about Shannon, how we're trying to stay close despite distance and bad feelings between me and Mom. We've made plans to see each other when we play at Red Bank in December. Now I'm wondering how I'll feel about my sister watching me ride the pines.

Everything I touch seems to turn to shit. Why? When will I start doing things right? Will it ever happen? Why couldn't *I* be coach's favorite? Why do *I* have these volcanoes on my face? Gerry says feeling sorry for yourself is pointless, that there are always people who have it far worse, that we should accept our lives with thanks and make the most of them. He's right, as usual, but that doesn't make me feel any better.

I pray a little bit. Most days I believe in God and admire Jesus, though it bugs me when the holy faction at Highview offers to save my soul and make Jesus my personal savior. For some reason it makes me think of Jesus as a personal trainer, and I picture him up there on the cross doing leg lifts and pull-ups and encouraging his disciples to *Feel the Burn*!

Sometimes we talk religion over at The High Court. We had an interesting discussion about what God would be on a basketball team. Danny thought He'd be a power forward, strong and tough and protective of His teammates. Angelo through He'd be a point guard, directing the action and tempo and making sure everyone was involved. Thaddeus thought He'd be a big dominating center, always reliable, taking over when the game was on the line. They laughed when I said I thought God would be the trainer, tending our wounds so we could get back in the game.

I stay up in the tree house a long time, warm enough in my sweatshirt and jacket. Then I push my bike up the hill to Granny's, flip on the spotlight, strip off my jacket, grab my outdoor ball, and shoot around. A half-hour later Granny comes outside with her winter coat over her robe.

"A bit on the cool side to be shooting in just a sweatshirt, isn't it?"

"It's okay, I'll come inside in a minute."

"Tough day?"

"Real tough," I say, struggling to control my voice.

"Want to talk? I could heat up some hot chocolate."

I'm tempted to say no, deal with my own problems as usual. But I suppose some talk will be okay, especially with Granny. She makes all the bad things seem like temporary blips. I shrug and we go inside, to the warmth of the kitchen.

ELEVEN

*I don't think about my dunk shots. I just
make sure I have a place to land.*

—Julius Erving,
The Book of Basketball Wisdom

I'm running free on the left wing, angling to the hoop
on a fast break. I take the pass and dribble once and
plant my right foot to take off for a lay-up when suddenly
my leg goes out from under me and I slide out of bounds
into the front row. The ref blows his whistle, and as I pull
myself up I notice he's wearing skates and a helmet. I run
back on defense, slipping a few times on the ice-covered
court. My man is wearing skates and goes right around

*me as I slip and struggle to keep my feet. I take short steps
so I don't fall again. When I get the ball, I try to make a
move, a crossover change of direction at the top of the key,
and I almost end up doing the splits. My hip bangs pain-
fully into the ice as I go down and lose the ball for the
second time. My teammates yell and curse and I wonder
why I haven't been given a pair of skates . . .*

Another weird one. I think about it during school a few
times, but can only figure that it has something to do with
my lack of control in recent basketball matters. I don't
know what to do about Moran's proposal. After second
period I decide that I definitely won't go out. After fourth
I decide that maybe I'll go out. I don't know what the hell
to do, and I can't think about much else.

After school I plan to borrow Granny's car and go
over to Danny's for some hoops and Monday Night Football. Granny said I could keep the car overnight and take
it to school in the morning. I don't borrow her car often
because I don't like leaving her stranded, but she insisted,
saying there was no where she wanted to go. Before I leave,
she gives me a grocery list and asks me to go shopping
for her tomorrow afternoon. Usually I spend a day or two
every week over at Danny's, sharing his basement apart-
ment. We get along great, like we've always been friends,
and I think we just might be friends until we're old men.

His occasional spontaneous moments with his girlfriend, Rachel, are my only concern. I don't mind, not at

all, but Rachel seems pretty possessive of his time. And she's a little chilly to me sometimes.

"She's not scheduled on Mondays, and Thursdays are soft," Danny laughed when I mentioned that I might have been cutting into their time. "Those are your nights here, Jax. But once in a while she just can't resist my studly body, so I hope you're cool with that."

I am cool with that. When she arrives on those nights, I talk with them for a couple minutes, then go shoot around under the spotlight. Sometimes Mr. Larson hears the patter of the ball and comes out to shoot a few himself.

I wondered if he knew what was going on with Danny and Rachel, and he answered the unasked question early in the summer. "That's one horny son-of-a-gun I got for a boy, ain't he, Jackson?" he said, tossing up his two-handed set shot with a feathery touch. "When are you gonna find yourself a girl? You're not a fag, are ya?"

When I arrive this afternoon, the guys are sprawled on cars off to the side of the court, carelessly caressing basketballs and telling stories. Danny is telling about a pep talk he received earlier in the day from Gowans, the Shoreview coach. He's a local legend in basketball circles, maybe even a state legend. His coaching style is based on the gospel of fundamentals, and he managed to spread the word down through the grade schools in Shoreview, so the kids learned the basics before they picked up bad habits from watching the NBA and playing ratball in the local schoolyards.

"Coach Gowans told me I gotta watch your ass this year," Danny says to Thaddeus. "I was tempted to say I'd leave that up to the lady spectators, but I knew he'd make me do extra sprints when we start practice."

"I can watch out for my own ass," Thaddeus comments.

"Well, Coach says people are going to be gunning for you, taking cheap shots, and I have to be your 'guardian angel.' I swear, he called me a guardian angel."

"Just my luck to get a white guardian angel," Thaddeus jokes. "You can bet the first hacker you knock on his butt ain't gonna think you're no angel, Danny. Nice to know Coach G. is looking out for me, though."

Even in the privacy of The High Court, the Shoreview players refer to him as Coach G. or Coach Gowans, and their respect is obvious. Angelo is the only player who has ever been disrespectful to Coach Gowans, and that was a result of a slip of the lip in the heat of battle. It happened last year when Shoreview was in a close game with Point Pleasant. As Angelo was dribbling up the court, Gowans motioned him over to the bench for instructions. Angelo's attention was diverted for a moment, and a quick guard took the opportunity to swipe the ball and sprint in for a lay-up.

Ever the competitor, Angelo was pissed. As he brought the ball up the court following the turnover, he glared over at Gowans and yelled, "Don't talk to me when I'm fucking dribbling!"

Even now, a year later, it's a running joke. At least once a night during our pickup games, someone will say, "Hey, don't talk to me when I'm fucking dribbling!"

I love listening to their Gowans stories, and wish I was playing for the man. Thaddeus tells another one about Gowans and the charge drill. He actually has a drill in which a player dribbles in from halfcourt and tries to hit a lay-up by running right through a defender planted under the basket.

"So one day last season we're doing the charge drill, right, and who do I get but Danny," Thaddeus says, lightly shoving Danny on one of his muscular shoulders. "No one wants to get Danny in the charge drill, you gotta be nuts. I wasn't paying attention or I would've switched places with a sophomore."

"I love plowing over sophomores," Danny interrupts. "Is there anything sweeter than running over underclassmen?"

"Anyway," Thaddeus continues, "I see Danny kind of smile and he starts dribbling toward me, picking up steam. Well I'm a man, I'm gonna take the shot, but I'm not stupid. I cover my Prized Possession with my hands." He demonstrates by folding his hands over his crotch.

Danny is laughing. "I hit Fly so hard I thought he was going to sail out of the gym. But he didn't even go down, just sort of staggered back a few steps until he regained his balance." This was said with admiration. Danny's victims usually peel themselves off the floor great distances from the point of impact.

Thaddeus says, "So Coach comes running up to me saying, 'No, no, no, no! You never cover your balls when you take a charge! The ref sees you take a Converse in the jewels, he's gonna call the foul! You got no balls if you cover your balls!' Well, I'm thinking, Yeah, and I got no balls if I get kneed in the balls by Danny, either. But I didn't say nothing because I didn't wanna do extra laps."

Angelo takes up the story. "So Coach is really rolling, using Thaddeus as an example, and he notices Fly didn't fall down when he took the charge. So he says, 'Thaddeus, you got to fall down when you get hit! Take it in the jewels, then fall down, fall down, fall down!' So Thaddeus is standing there nodding with the rest of us, and he keels over backwards like he'd been shot. Nobody wanted to laugh, but we couldn't help it. Even Coach Gowans was smiling a little, but he made us run."

"Yeah, I felt bad about that, guys," Thaddeus says, extracting himself from his car. "Just couldn't help it. Humor of the situation and all."

We start shooting around. Angelo asks us to clear the middle and he does his running-up-the-wall dunk. Because he's so short, it's easy to overlook his athletic ability. He's quicker than any player I've ever seen, hands and feet a blur of motion the entire game, and he's almost as fast as Thaddeus despite his stumpy legs. Plus, his body is rock hard with muscle. We've all made the mistake of bringing the ball down too low after a rebound and had Angelo snatch it away. He steals it so fast that sometimes you don't even realize it happened, and you start to pass something you're no longer holding.

Danny and I follow Angelo with some slams of our own. I'm almost eye level with the rim when I throw mine down. We wait for Thaddeus to take his turn—he never uses the wall, of course—but he's off to the side with a strange look on his face.

"Jackson," he says, "I think you can dunk."

"'Course I can," I laugh. "You just saw that."

"No, for real, not this wall cheating stuff."

"I don't think so."

"When was the last time you tried?"

"Pickup game after school a couple of weeks ago. I was trying to impress Coach Moran, who was kind of checking out the action, and I almost threw it down, but it bounced off the back rim, and he yelled at me for trying to show-boat. Haven't tried since."

"Well, I don't want to give you a big head, but you take some rebounds at rim level or above, and that's going off two feet. Going off one you should be able to slam."

So I shrug, grab the ball, and head to the right side of the court. Everyone clears off to the top area near the tree. Being lefty, I run down the middle from a forty-five degree angle, leap off my strong right leg, and try to put her home. I leave the ground strongly, cup the ball, clear the rim and swing it down. The ball nips the front of the rim, skids across to the back, and bounces out.

"Close," Danny says.

"Thought you had it," Angelo echoes.

"Couple of things, Jax," Thaddeus says. Unlike most great players, who tend to be self-absorbed, Thaddeus is very patient when teaching basketball. We all think he'll make a good coach some day, and I've mentioned it a few times, but he shrugs off the compliment, says it's too far down the line to think about. "First, look at this scuff mark, see that?" A black mark about six inches long is slashed across The High Court's dark gray surface. "That's where you dragged your left foot. You lost a couple of inches right there. And after dragging your foot, you're not driving your left knee up hard enough. That's another inch or two. Basically, your left side is all messed up. Here, give the ball to Uncle Thaddeus, practice a couple of times without it."

I feel silly but follow instructions. It takes three tries not to drag my left foot, and another two before I combine a clean takeoff with the proper knee thrust. I get it right, and I touch the front of the rim well below my wrist, my fingertips maybe nine inches above the rim.

I look over at Thaddeus, smiling and amazed, and he shakes his head and laughs into his hand. "What?" I ask. "Did you see me soar on that one, Fly? I did it right, didn't I?"

"Yeah, you got it, man," he says. "No offense, Jax. I'm laughing 'cause, well, I wouldn't have to explain how to jump to a brother, you know what I'm saying?" He tosses me the ball. "Now go for it."

I get the takeoff right and stuff the ball easily, like I've been doing it for years. Angelo, Danny, and Thaddeus let out a collective roar and tackle me and pummel my back and mess with my hair. "You're a damn dunker now, Jackson!" Danny screams. "A damn dunker on The High Court!"

"And this is asphalt!" Angelo says. "Off a wood floor, you're going to be doing tomahawks!" With that, they carry me over to Danny's car and plop me down on the hood hard enough to make a dent. Danny is so pumped he doesn't mind a bit.

I hop right off, grab the ball, and say what I guess every player says after his first dunk: "Let me try that again!"

Focusing on my takeoff, I dunk again with ease. It was not a fluke. The second roar brings Mr. Larson out of the store, wondering why all the screaming, and he smiles proudly at me when Danny tells him about the dunks. "Feel up to an encore performance for an old fan?" he asks.

"Sure," I say. Confident now, I drift in easily, clear the rim, then violently slam the ball down at the last moment before starting to come down, which adds to the drama.

"Holy cow!" Mr. Larson says. "You jumped like a nig . . . like a black man on that dunk, Jackson."

"Not quite like a nigger," Thaddeus says, winking at Mr. Larson. "But not bad."

I look up at the vibrating hoop and raise my fists in salute. A primal scream erupts from my throat. I've seen dunks bring smiles to a lot of faces over the years, to dozens of guys with better hops than me. And now I'm part of the club, the small group of humans who know the power and joy of the dunk.

I put it down a few dozen times, postponing the game and bringing on cramps in my calves. I'm an addict of altitude, a junkie of the jam. I thank Thaddeus over and over and can't stop smiling. I have no problems. And I vow to slam over every Jagoff in the gym when I go out for the team.

TWELVE

*Put anything under pressure and you'll bring
out what's inside.*

—Pat Riley, as quoted in *My Life*
by Magic Johnson with William Novak

Last night, in celebration of an excellent first day of practice, during which I dunked over three Jagoffs, I gave into temptation and downed a decadent hot fudge sundae with nuts. So I have no one to blame but myself for the fresh volcanoes on my chin and neck this morning.

A couple of years ago a dermatologist told me with a straight face that diet had nothing to do with acne. Others have since confirmed this so-called fact and cited scientific studies. I wonder exactly how the studies were conducted—did they feed candy bars to lab rats, maybe?—because they are seriously stupid.

I've conducted my own studies since my skin broke out when I was thirteen, and I know, for example, that a zit will appear and begin to grow on my chin exactly twenty-two minutes after I consume anything with nuts. While I admit that I don't understand the zit-forming process as well as dermatologist, I know this Dr. Jekyll-Nut and Mr. Hyde-My-Face transformation is very real, and I kind of resent them telling me it's not true. My common sense and experience tell me otherwise. I also know my skin reacts in an hour to chocolate, two hours to dairy products. Very predictable and very depressing. How can something that tastes so good become something that looks so ugly?

Anyway, I have a zit ritual that I perform first thing in the morning and last thing at night. I begin the morning ritual by washing my face with special zit soap. Then I clean the volcanic remnants with the special zit disinfectant. Then I help the newly formed volcanoes to a premature eruption, a slightly pleasurable release of pressure—pop!—that sends a magma of whiteheads and oily blood splattering across the mirror.

Pretty gross, I know.

(While on the subject of pleasurable releases, I will add that I also whack off. But while I don't mind discussing my volcanic acne, the sexual subject is off limits. I read that old book *Portnoy's Complaint*, and was amazed at the details the writer included about whacking off. He'd obviously conducted years of research. But I think it's enough to admit I whack off frequently and skip the in-depth descriptions. Basically, I see it as a private matter between me and my Good Buddy.)

Now to get back to the ritual. After cleaning the mirror, I wash my face again and disinfect the freshly squeezed zits. Then I shave. I started shaving last year, and it's a very delicate procedure when you have zits. To get the hairs you have to slide the razor up the slopes of the volcanoes, but not over the summit. Nick the sensitive, freshly erupted crater with a blade and you have a bloody mess that won't dry up until second period.

Following the shave, I wash the cream off my face with hot water, throw on some cold, and pat dry. Then I smear the Clearasil onto the bloomers. I use the invisible stuff. The other type, which supposedly disguises your zits by matching your skin color, doesn't work for me because my volcanoes are major mountains. A bag over my head would work better.

The final step in the morning ritual is to name the new formations. As a sophomore I wrote a research paper for English class on volcanoes, and was struck by the similarities between these pressure valves on the earth's surface and those on my skin's surface. Even the vocabulary worked. I'm talking about *eruption* and *magma* and *crater* and *spatter cones*. These were not just words to me, but things I witnessed daily on a smaller scale. I scored an A on the paper.

My worst volcanoes were the Vesuvius on my neck last spring, and the Krakatoa alongside my nose over the summer. Both erupted for days and took weeks to disappear. They're gone now, but I'm afraid they may be merely dormant, not extinct.

Nothing quite so serious today, just a Popo on my chin and Fuji on my forehead. Of more concern are Shasta and Rainier, on the left and right sides of my neck, respectively. These are extinct formations that have left large, lumpy scars. They are symmetrically located, and I've heard a couple of wise-ass comments about "Frankenstein," referring to my size and those electrodes sticking out the sides of the monster's neck, in the same general area as my scars.

I keep hoping Rainier and Shasta will disappear along with my active acne some day soon, but I know that scars just don't go away, and that they'll be an ugly reminder that I'll have to look at the rest of my life.

I also hope I'm through with major volcanoes. The ritual and watching my diet helps, I know. The situation seems to be improving slightly. Still, I sometimes worry that a Mount St. Helens is in there waiting, biding its time until I work up my courage to ask out a girl.

So far the embarrassment about my skin has overcome my courage. I can sort of see girls looking at my zits when they look at me, and it makes me feel like one big pustular freak.

Usually I have a new volcano or two to deal with in the evening, too. Sweat from my daily workouts, while healthy overall, doesn't help my skin situation. So I repeat my morning ritual, except for the shaving. I try to sleep on my back so I don't get the Clearasil on my pillow case, but it never works. I end up rolling over during the night, and I stain and ruin a lot of pillow cases. I worry that Granny thinks I use them for other purposes, but I'm not that inconsiderate.

In her sensitive way, Granny brought up the topic of my pimples, and offered to take me to a dermatologist. My mom sends me a couple hundred bucks a month, which is plenty for my usual expenses, but not enough to cover a dermatologist, too. And I told Granny about my prior experience with dermatologists, about their stupid research and drugs that didn't help. Once she got me talking, I told her everything. About how embarrassed I was by my zits, and about how I hated the idea of being scarred for life.

She patted my hand and told me not to worry, that I was going to be a good-looking man even if I had some scars. "Look at the actor Tommy Lee Jones," she said. "He has acne scars, but he's a fine-looking fellow all the same. Scars on a man are not as important as you think."

Maybe she's right. In any case, Granny is the human version of a basketball court, making me feel okay even when everything sucks.

THIRTEEN

Once you've made it to a court, your next challenge is to get into a game. For many beginning players (and veterans as well), the most unsavory element of a trip to a new court is finding a way to get on it.

—Chris Ballard, *Hoops Nation*

I always like visiting Red Bank, especially during the Christmas season. As the bus carries the team across the Navesink River, I think back on all the fun times we had shopping. We'd walk along looking at the lights and displays, then Dad would give Shannon and me some money and let us roam the stores. We'd haul our bags of gifts into the designated meeting place two hours later and share hot chocolate.

Red Bank has a good team, according to the paper. No match for Shoreview, but better than us. Most likely our first game of the year will be a loss. A major concern is their front line, a bunch of strong six-five football types. They out-rebounded every team they played last year, and that's good news for me. I might get some serious minutes if one of the Jagoffs fails to box out under the boards.

We're taking lay-ups when I spot Shannon and a couple of her freshmen friends under the basket. I take my lay-up and give her a quick hug. "Mom couldn't make it," she says apologetically.

"No problem," I shrug, and jog back to the end of the rebounding line. I wonder why she couldn't make it, if I did something to make her mad. She seems mad at me whenever I talk to her or see her, and now she doesn't bother to come to the game. Sometimes I get the feeling she doesn't want me as a son anymore.

Shannon's taller and slimmer since the summer. Could pass for a junior, maybe. The baby fat on her face is gone, and her hair is cut short in a swept back style, rather than hanging in the pigtails of her junior high days. The thin scar under her chin is barely noticeable. Her dark eyes are a contrast to her light complexion, and they complete a face that is, I suddenly realize, really beautiful. My little sister, a young hottie.

More than ever I wish I was around to be her big brother, look out for her. And just talk to her in person more than every couple of months. I watch her take a seat in the third row of the stands—on the Red Bank side—and it seems she's surrounded by a dozen or more friends, including a few attentive guys. She looks happy.

Of course I'm embarrassed to take my seat on the bench at the beginning of the game. I'm very anxious for one of the Jagoffs to screw up so I can play. My ideal season has gone down the drain, but I'm hoping I can do well when I'm in games, maybe impress Moran into giving me more court time.

A few minutes into the game Michaels throws a pass away and gives up an offensive rebound, and I'm leaning forward, ready to head to the scorer's table. But Coach Moran doesn't call my name. He sends in a sophomore instead, and I feel my face getting hot.

The second quarter passes the same way. We're down ten at the half, and I'm pissed but trying to hide it as I listen to Moran lecture about boxing out and playing better defense. When he excuses himself to take a dump, Stoner walks over and sits next to me.

"What did you do to get on his bad side today?" he asks.

"Nothing, at least nothing I can think of."

"The girl you hugged is your sister?"

"Yeah."

"This sucks. Why don't you talk to him? Find out what's up? You've been dominating in practice, dude. We need you."

"Ah, I don't know. I don't think so." Stoner shrugs and goes out the back door for a quick joint. We're not good enough friends for me to confide that I would probably lose it and start crying in front of Moran or, worse, take a swing at him.

I don't play in the second half, either. I catch Shannon looking across at me a few times, with a concerned expression. I pretend to be absorbed in the game. I don't even get minutes during garbage time when we're down by eighteen. I remember Thaddeus telling me I'm not good enough to be cool, so I don't pull any theatrics like putting a towel over my head. I just sit there and take it. The only positive thing is that my mother isn't here to witness my humiliation.

I don't need a shower, so after Coach Moran gives a brief "We'll Get 'Em at Our Place" speech, I head back to the court. Shannon is still sitting with her friends, and I force myself to walk over despite my shame.

"Jackson, are you hurt?" she says when I get close. That's my little sis, giving me an out. She wouldn't mind if I lied to save face, and it's tempting. I could even throw in a convincing limp. But I remember my promise to Gerry about improving my relationship with reality, so I say, "No, Coach just didn't put me in."

"They could have used you," one of the guys says, trying to boost me by cutting down my team.

"Yeah, looked like you had a good jumper," another kid smirks. "In the warm-ups." He glances around, and I see he's trying to impress the girls and using me to show off his wit. He has no idea how close he is to a broken nose.

"My jumper's not bad," I say. A couple of balls are still rolling around the court. I set down my coat and gym bag and take off my sweater. "Feed me a few, will you?" I ask the smirking kid, and he shrugs and walks toward the basket.

I start in the left corner, behind the three-point line. The kid is standing in front of the basket. After I make three, moving with each shot a couple of steps around the semi-circle, I pause and say with cocky assurance, "Just stand right under the basket, they're all going in." And they do, one after another, as I continue around the arc to the opposite corner. I miss once on the way back, just barely. Most of my shots are draining right down the pipe into the kid's waiting hands. As I near the corner where I started, I notice some of the fans who were leaving have stopped to watch, and when I swish my last shot, there's a ripple of applause. A tall man walks over shaking his head.

"Lordy, lordy," he says smiling. "Why'd they keep you on the bench?"

"I don't know."

"Well, you got a beautiful jumper, son. You hang in there, don't get down on yourself. You can play college ball with that shot, no doubt about it."

"Thanks." My hand disappears into his as we shake, and I know he was a ballplayer once upon a time. The compliment and Shannon's proud face almost redeem the night, and I sit and talk with her until the bus is loaded with Jagoffs and ready to pull away.

All the way back to Highland I think about quitting the team. I wouldn't say anything to Moran, because I'm still too emotional. No, I'd just be a no-show at practice tomorrow and the next day, and tell him where to go if he dares to seek me out. Not that he would bother. After tonight, he'd know exactly why I quit.

I've more or less decided on that course of action when Moran calls me up to the front of the bus.

"You're mad at me, right, Jackson?"

I shrug. "I don't know."

"You look mad. You know why you didn't play tonight?"

"No."

"You didn't play because I'm trying to establish a unit among the starters, and I wanted to give our sophomores their first varsity experience. You'll play next game, spelling Chipper like we talked about. So keep your head up."

I want to tell him I quit, but I'm too cowardly. I nod, mumble okay, and slink back to my seat feeling worse than ever.

FOURTEEN

> *As a kid, I always had a ball with me. Always. I*
> *slept with the ball, I dribbled up and down the*
> *stairs, I set up a slalom course of cardboard boxes and*
> *dribbled through it as fast as I could . . . The funni-*
> *est thing was me dribbling when I took out the trash*
> *. . . At first I wasn't very good, and people in other*
> *apartments would be hanging out their windows*
> *and doors, watching me and laughing. I had trash*
> *spilling all over the place, and they'd be giving me*
> *all kinds of heck. But I had the last laugh. It wasn't*
> *long before I could make it all the way down to the*
> *dumpster without spilling a thing.*
>
> —Tyrone "Muggsy" Bogues and David
> Levine, *In the Land of Giants*

Christmas comes and goes in a wave of phony cheer. I find myself wearing a frozen smile when Granny and I go to visit Mom and Shannon in Red Bank and exchange gifts Christmas morning. I'm trying to make things nice, and so is Mom, but we're both still angry, and tension sort of wrecks the day. After I talk to Shannon for a while, I'm dying to go somewhere and shoot around. Finally Granny and Mom run out of conversation and

Granny says we should be going to Gerry's. Mom sort of half-hugs me goodbye, and we head out into the sunshine, to my relief.

On New Year's I go to a party over at the Larsons,' which peaks when Angelo runs across the backyard at midnight wearing only a Santa beard. His baring is getting more daring, and Danny and I are pretty worried.

I politely refuse drinks offered me, even though part of me feels like drowning my senior-season sorrows. After five games, I have a pathetic total of eleven points. Eleven points in five games, when I was planning to average sixteen a game. I was so anxious to prove myself to Moran the second game that I forced a couple of long jumpers, missing both. Then I missed three open outside shots. Then I started hesitating, thinking about it, and I haven't dared a jumper since. All my points have come on garbage around the hoop and one free throw—a three-point play on an offensive rebound that is my sole highlight. Moran keeps playing me the same nine or ten minutes because I'm doing a good job on the boards and defense, and I'm passing the ball to the Jagoffs.

At the party, I spin away from all attempts to talk to me about why my point totals are so low in the newspaper box scores. I bring the conversation around to Shoreview's undefeated season, which everyone wants to talk about, anyway.

I'm relieved when school starts again in early January. The first day back Gerry announces that we'll be starting a speech unit. We'll be reading great speeches and writing and delivering our own. He warmed us up for this by having us stand and read an excerpt from our journals once a week since the beginning of the school year.

Like most of the other students, I'm not crazy about speaking in front of the class, but I'm capable of handling it. Kelly and Marvin and a few others relish the opportunity to express themselves and seem completely relaxed during speeches. At the other extreme are a few super shy students who would rather be dragged by a car than speak in public.

Near the end of class, Gerry addresses the fear of public speaking. "Why do we get nervous when we have to give a speech in front of a bunch of people?" he asks.

"Because we're afraid of looking like an idiot," Branchflower says.

"Exactly," Gerry agrees. "And why do we fear that? Is it a natural fear, like the fear of falling?"

"Seems to be," Renker says. "At least for most people."

"Really? Think about a small child, who will instinctively throw up his arms if you pretend you're dropping him. But is that child afraid to crawl in front of a group of people and drool, spit, cry, and soil his diaper?"

"Heck no."

"So it follows that the child would not be afraid to speak, if he could. And you've probably seen young kids babble away in front of a group of people from time to time, with no self-consciousness whatsoever."

"Yeah," Christine says. "You learn as you get older that you don't want to make a fool out of yourself in front of others."

"Exactly, Christine," Gerry says. "The fear of speaking in public, while very common and very real, is an acquired fear. As we get older we learn—unfortunately, in my view—that people will ridicule us sometimes, that we should be ashamed of ourselves if we do something wrong or badly, or if we do something socially inappropriate. And after all that, many of us do not prize ourselves enough as human beings to stand in front of others and talk to them as equals. We acquire these fears as we acquire our egos, but it's really a fear based on a false assumption. The good news is"—here Gerry does his Yoda imitation—"you can unlearn the fear you've learned, young ones."

"Whaddaya mean, Master Yoda?" Renker asks.

"Let me tell you a story," Gerry continues with a smile. "In college I had a roommate named Ronny Sullivan, Sully for short. Well, for some reason Sully and I played this practical joke in which we'd run off with the other guy's towel and robe while he was in the shower, preferably when he had shampoo in his eyes. Usually the victim had to wait around and ask someone to borrow a towel. I know, pretty immature stuff, and I plead guilty.

"Anyway, this one time Sully came in and grabbed my towel and robe, and I couldn't wait around for help, I had a class to get to. So I sprinted down the hall after him, starko."

Nervous laughter rolls around the room. It's safe to say none of us ever heard a teacher confess to running naked down a hallway before. I make a mental note to tell Angelo this story. Next to me, Ivory Lewis leans forward and whispers to Kelly, loud enough for me to hear, "I would have paid to see that." Kelly snorts a little laugh of agreement.

"Problem was," Gerry continues, "that I had shampoo in my eyes. Now our room was the last on the right, and I almost made it there, but not quite. I was hoping to get there before he locked the door or put his weight against it—Sully was a big guy—so I quickly turned the handle and threw my shoulder into the door." He pauses for effect.

"Well, the door wasn't locked, and Sully wasn't on the other side, because I had the wrong room. It was our neighbor's room, and a meeting of the Residential Attendants was in session, four men and five women. They were voting on whether to make all the dorms co-ed, and here I am, flying across the room wearing nothing but a capful of Suave."

Now the class is really laughing. "Yeah, so much for Robert's Rules of Order," Gerry says. "I don't know if I influenced their decision, but it's a fact they voted to keep the men's and women's dorms separate. To say I was embarrassed is an understatement."

"Probably not the only understated thing in the room," Renker calls out.

"The point," Gerry continues over the laughter, "is that this was the most embarrassing moment of my life, and probably more embarrassing than anything any of you will ever do. And you know what? It wasn't that bad. Embarrassment is just your ego overreacting to unfamiliar sensory input. When we screw up publicly, we're practically trained to blush, apologize, smile stupidly, explain inanely, and leave quickly. Which is exactly what I did following my bold entrance into dorm politics. But I've learned a few things since then. If it happened today, I like to think I'd say, 'Excuse me, wrong room,' and walk calmly out the door."

"How could you?"

"By not getting in your own way. Everyone in that room, everyone in this room, has done something embarrassing, right? We all step out of formation or pull a faux pas from time to time, so what's the big deal? You're not required to feel shameful about such moments. You can observe the stress on yourself rather than falling prey to it."

Cool blue eyes survey the room under his mop of curly tan hair, and Gerry seems to wonder if his message is getting through. "Try that when you give your speeches," he says. "Observe the stress you feel when facing a group of people you have to talk to. Breathe deeply, let the stress pass through your system in silence, knowing it's based on false and silly fear. And then give your speech."

The quiet voice of Jeannie Nash asks, "What if we can't get rid of the fear?"

"Trust me, Jeannie, you will. Each speech you give will get easier. And let's start getting this absurd feeling of embarrassment out of the way right now. Then, when you get up to speak, you won't have to worry about it."

He looks around the room for a victim. "Marvin Renker, on your feet."

"Yes sir, me Capitan!" Renker says, leaping off the couch in back and saluting briskly.

"Marvin, I'd like you to recite the first sentence of the Gettysburg Address while holding your tongue between your thumb and forefinger. I know you don't have it memorized, so I've written it down for you."

He hands over the card. Renker readies himself. "Thor sore an sweven ears a row," he begins, and laughter stops him.

"Marvin, you just made a fool out of yourself," Gerry says when the noise subsides. "Think you can live through it? Think anyone will have a lower opinion of you because of your performance? I mean, lower than they already have?"

"Cheap shot, Mr. D!" Renker says. "But yeah, I think I'll live through it, and I don't think anyone will think less of me."

"Thanks, Marvin, that's why I selected you first. I know a confident person when I see one."

Next he convinces Kelly to give an impromptu speech about being a rabbit while hopping around the room. Several more students readily agree to appear foolish before we notice the time and start to pack up, still smiling.

"Think of a how-to speech topic for next class," Gerry says. "We'll have five speakers a day, beginning next week. Minimum of three minutes, maximum of four. And I don't want any 'How to Roll a Blunt' speeches or 'How Not to Give a Speech' speeches, got it? Remember, everyone, the key to delivering a good speech, and many other things is life, is to practice, practice, practice."

FIFTEEN

To our way of thinking, the Indians' symbol is the circle, the hoop. Nature wants things to be round. The bodies of human beings and animals have no corners. With us the circle stands for the togetherness of people who sit with one another around the campfire.

—John Lame Deer, *Seeker of Visions*

Tonight I'm over at Danny's, reading Phil Jackson's book *Sacred Hoops* and semi-watching the Knicks lose to Miami. I'm halfway annoyed when Danny snatches the book out of my hands.

"Ah, the Zen master on the ways of basketball," he says. "Wonder if everyone would think he's such hot stuff if he was coaching in Memphis and Denver rather than Chicago and L.A."

"Not so easy to keep those big egos working toward a common goal," I say.

"Well, I'm prejudiced against Jackson. My old man never liked him when he was on the Knicks, he was a Bradley and DeBusshere man. Said in one year Jackson went from Action Jackson to Filthy Phil, your basic hack off the bench."

"He's a champion both as a player and coach," I suggest. "Can't take that from him."

Danny shrugs and heads over to his dresser. He distracts me from my divided attention when he stands in front of his full-length mirror in his boxer shorts and sprays perfume directly into his face. I can't quite believe what I'm seeing. One of my friends runs around naked, and the other is using perfume. "What the hell, Danny!"

"Yeah, I'm putting some of Rachel's perfume under my nose. I think it's called Ode de something."

"Something is rotten in the state of Danny world when he starts wearing his girl's perfume. I mean, correct me if I'm wrong, but she's supposed to wear the perfume, big guy."

"I got another bottle for her, so she lent me this half-full one," he says. "I use less than her."

"I sure hope so. You're kinda scaring me here, Danny."

He turns, his face serious. "It's not to wear, Jax. It's for my nose."

"You're snorting your girlfriend's perfume? I think there are support groups for that. Maybe a twelve-step thing. You should enroll before people start to talk."

"Is there a program for feet?" he asks. "No offense, Jackson, but your feet are the worst things I've ever smelled, and I've smelled all sorts of rotten fish down by the pier, and I once hugged a toilet bowl for two hours after drinking and puking my first bottle of Jack Daniels."

I'm insulted. My mouth is open wide enough for a few slices of Sal's pizza. "Sorry," I say. "Look, if it's that bad, I can stay at Granny's all the time."

"See, I knew you'd get defensive!" he yells, marching over to his bed and sitting down across from me. "I like having you here, dude. You're my best friend. I just need to dab a little perfume under my nostrils to neutralize your foot odor. I'm being honest, okay?"

"Your feet don't smell like flowers."

"Mine stink after a workout, for sure, but I'm not in your league in the foot odor department. Seriously, Jax, you should see a doctor or something. All the sweat in your body comes out your feet."

"And all that air in your brain comes out your mouth!"

"Hey, bite me, okay? I'm trying to help you out, and here you are snapping my head off!"

"What do you expect? You're cutting me down, I'm just defending myself."

"My point exactly. Stop defending yourself and listen. Here, I'll paint you a picture." He uses his hands to aid his imagery. "You meet this great woman, okay? Breasts out to here, gorgeous face, long legs, the whole package. And she's digging you. She whispers in your ear she wants to go somewhere and hook up. So you take her to your place, wherever."

"Could happen."

"Yeah, definitely. So anyway, you start kissing. It's getting hot. You lose your shirt, she loses hers. Then you take off your shoes and she sprints for the door, screaming."

Before I can think of a comeback, Angelo knocks and strolls into the basement eating a calzone. "What's up?" he asks around the cheese and sausage. "I could hear you guys yelling all the way over at Sal's."

"We're having an argument about Jackson's incredibly smelly feet," Danny says.

"Yeah, Danny just informed me that girls don't like smelly feet. I'll tell you, Angelo, I was amazed. Who would have thought that? You must be a genius, Danny. All this time I thought girls didn't like me because of my zits, and it was my feet I should have been worried about."

"They don't like sarcastic smart-asses, either."

"Actually," Angelo says, wiping his hands, "I heard that something in male perspiration turns girls on."

"See?" I say. "All I have to do is take off my shoes and socks and they'll be tearing off the rest of my clothes."

"Didn't hurt me," Angelo continues. "You know that pickup game we had last week, when we drew the nice crowd of hot young things? Well, I hooked up after with that sophomore, Debbie. And I was dripping with sweat."

"Saw you talking to her," Danny says. "But hooked up how, exactly?"

"Hooked up majorly. "

"You lie," Danny says.

Instead of protesting and trying to convince us, Angelo just shrugs. Danny and I look at each other in confusion. Usually Angelo would have been off on a highly descriptive tale of sexual conquest. Now he just wears a little smile.

"Wow," I say, "you actually had a good reason to get naked?"

"Yup."

"This could work out well for you, Angelo," Danny says. "We've been worried about you getting arrested for public indecency. But having an actual girl in the picture changes things. The cops will no longer think you're an exhibitionist, just another horny high school guy."

"Hey, before you cartoons really get rolling, let me tell you that I like this girl, okay? I really like her. So don't be talking trash about her."

"You're the one who started talking about majorly hooking up with a sophomore while sweating profusely," Danny points out.

"Okay, that's true, and I shouldn't have. Except you guys have never, ever believed me before, so I couldn't resist telling you this time."

"So all the other times were lies?" Danny asks.

"Slight exaggerations."

"Uh-huh," I say. "So when Melanie supposedly . . ."

"Don't go there, Jax, or I'll start talking about your Irish-cursed little buddy, and the fact that your feet *do* stink."

"Great, criticism from a miniature exhibitionist, that's all I need."

At this point Danny steps in like a ref. "Come on, guys, we're all friends here, right?"

I regret the cheap shots so I apologize to Angelo. "Hope it works out with you and Debbie, really," I say.

"Thanks, Jax," Angelo says. "And I hope your foot odor and zits clear up sometime."

"Hey, I said I was sorry!"

"I owed you one."

"That was two!"

"Since we're on a Jackson roll, I have a third," Danny says. When I cover my face with a pillow, he adds, "Jax, buddy, my basement bachelor pad is not the place to hang out if you're looking to inflate your self-esteem. This is a palace of truth, justice, and the American way."

"Thanks, Superman. Fire when ready."

"Okay, you have to stop staring at breasts."

My mouth drops open again. The sudden shift from zits to tits puts me in shock. "And you guys don't stare at breasts?"

"Not the way you do," Danny continues. "Sure, we check 'em out, but on the sly. Angela has mentioned that she's caught you checking hers out pretty blatantly a few times."

I'm blushing and about to angrily deny it. A wave of embarrassment is washing over me, then I remember Gerry's advice to look it in the eye and watch it fade away. "Tell her it's a compliment," I say, and immediately feel better.

"Yeah, I really don't think she minded much. The point is, she noticed."

"Maybe she was wrong," Angelo says. "I've noticed that Jackson's feet stink, but I haven't seen him stare at breasts more than any other dude."

"Thanks, Angelo."

"No problem."

"Besides," I add, "girls don't notice guys checking out their hooters."

"How do you know?" Danny asks.

"I've never been told by a girl to stop checking her out."

"That's no kind of evidence," Danny says. "You know what we need, guys? An experiment."

I see a problem right off. "What girl is going to admit she noticed us staring? Or want to hang with us ever again if we subject her to the experiment?"

"Good point," Danny says. After a few seconds of thought, he snaps his fingers. "Got it. We'll use Marty."

"He does have a big chest," Angelo says.

Marty is Danny's little brother. He's a freshman, a nice guy, very smart, and not too athletic. He's a little overweight and naturally big through the upper body, like all the Larson men. We only ask Marty to play hoops with us if we're really desperate for bodies.

Angelo goes to get our unsuspecting lab rat, who follows him down the steps. "What's going on?" Marty asks.

"Nothing, bro," Danny says. "Just wondering how you're enjoying your first year of high school?"

"Oh, it's okay," he says, pleased with the attention. "I like most of the classes, except gym. I wish Shoreview was more academically oriented. Can you believe they want to spend a million bucks on a new football field, and yet they don't have enough science books to go around? I'm gonna write an editorial, and not just for the school paper . . . Hey, why are you guys looking at my chest?"

We stop staring at his imaginary breasts and look at each other. A truth dawns, and we express it as one: "They know!"

SIXTEEN

Though everyone should live alone at some
time in a life . . . It can be all right.
You can end up more within yourself, as the
best athletes are, which is worth it.
(A basketball player who goes for his patented
outside jumper becomes nothing more than
the simple wish personified that the
ball go in the hole.)

—Richard Ford, *The Sportswriter*

When I come home after practice the next afternoon, Granny is waiting in the kitchen, wearing
her serious expression, the one she usually has in church.
She seems to realize this and smiles as she says, casually
as possible, "A letter came for you, Jackson. From California." She hands me the letter. I want to rip it open
and read it immediately, but control my curious impulse
out of respect for Granny. We talk about school and the

weather. The first real snow of the year has fallen and cars are sliding off the roads and sometimes into each other.

Finally I head to my room and open the letter.

Dear Jackson,

I'm sorry I haven't called you or contacted you sooner. Funny, they told us in the program that we need to stop apologizing, stop feeling guilty, and move forward with our lives. Easier said than done when you look back on the ruin you've caused, but I see the point. You feel badly and want to feel better, and the easiest way is to have another drink, then another, then swear to start fresh tomorrow. The drinks dull the pain until the next morning, when you're right back where you started, and have the demons of a hangover to contend with as well.

Writing letters is out of style, I know. I know you have e-mail and a phone, but indulge my old-fashioned ways, this one is harmless enough. As you know, my other old-fashioned ways are not so harmless, they are what caused the problems, along with the drinking. I come from a New York neighborhood, Jackson, where most people have rigid ideas about how to live. You are Catholic and go to church weekly as a boy, at least a few times a year as a man, and require your wife to go rather more often. You can trace your family back to the Old Sod and know what your ancestors did. As a boy you play hard, as a man you work word. And a man is a "real" man—he drinks, he smokes, he fights.

Looking over what I've just written, I realize it sounds ridiculous. A man who lovingly takes care of his family but refrains from drinking, smoking, and fighting wouldn't be considered much of a man in my neighborhood, and that's not right. But while I recognize this as wrong, I know damn well I would have been one of those sitting on the bar stool laughing with the boys about the hen-pecked choir boy who won't take a drink and thinks he's better than everyone because he doesn't indulge in the neighborhood's preferred vices. I'm ashamed to admit I was involved in such discussions a few times in my younger years.

My counselor out here has taken me apart and put me back together again, explained my twisted thinking and gone-to-hell judgment, and yet the habits of thought are so ingrained I have a hard time dismissing them from my mind. I have to think it through step by step before I can see clearly. And every step hurts.

One of the reasons I moved us away from the neighborhood when I made a few bucks was that I wanted a different life for you all. Maybe deep down I realized the values of the old neighborhood were twisted and destructive, although this is the first time I've admitted as much.

Did I ever tell you about how you got your name, son? Must have, though I can't remember. It was because you are "Jack's son." Pretty clever of me, huh? I was so proud the day you were born, and so in love with your mother. I remember being determined, burning with determination. I was going to be the perfect husband and father. The best lawyer in New York. I was going to be the man I envisioned becoming, a great family man, famous in my circle, popular, the image of success. And I'd still be a regular guy from the neighborhood when I was passing through.

Obviously things didn't work out the way I had planned. Guess it doesn't for most drunks, maybe most people. If you don't die first, you could go broke, or lose your wife, or lose your kids, or lose your partnership in the firm. Or in my case, all of the above.

The day I hit bottom is very easy to finger. Looking back, it seems like a dream—a nightmare—and something I just could not have done in real life. The root idea, I think, was to show you where I come from. In the bar when we talked it over, it didn't seem like a bad idea. Now I just don't understand how I could think that way. There are many things I don't understand about my behavior the last few years, that hurt when I look back and confront. My counselor tells me that I control my mind and don't have to watch the horror flicks that lurk there, and most days I'm strong enough to walk past that particular theater. Other days, though, it seems that if I don't look, I'm pretending it never happened, and that doesn't seem right. But sure enough, the days I watch the bad movies are the days I feel most thirsty.

I haven't yielded to my alcohol cravings for six months. Today is my half-year anniversary of being sober, and I'm proud of myself . . . I know what you're thinking. I went into the program over a year ago, why have I been dry just six months? The truth is I was dry for two months when I got out, then had a bad day. I had a good two weeks, then a bad three days. A couple of more slips, and then I started steadfastly down my recovery road, which has no end, they tell me.

There is always a good excuse to have a few drinks, I've found. I have been very lonely, and that's my best excuse, the one I pull out most frequently before slipping it quietly back in the drawer. For a while I harbored the illusion that I might be able to repair the damaged relationship with your mother, which was stupid thinking, as she bluntly put it. I haven't met any other women, haven't been looking much to tell the truth. It's hard to socialize when you're in your late forties. You can't fall into a crowd of fun people the way you can when you're younger.

My financial situation is still shaky, but improving. My company covered the expense of the clinic last year and kept me on salary, which was good of them. Then they fired me as soon as I completed the program, which was not. I've been working as a temp lawyer, close to forty hours most weeks, and I'm doing well and hoping to catch on full-time with a firm that's been using me on a regular basis. The pay is good, but most goes to your mother for support, as you know. I don't resent that, but

I wish I were making more money. At the very least I would like to take better care of you all financially. She told me she's sending you $200 a month. With basketball, I don't imagine you have time to work, so I'd like to supplement your allowance a bit when I land a good job, if you'll let me.

I wanted to tell you that I'm glad to be alive, Jackson. For the first time in six or seven years, I'm really glad to be alive. Every morning I take an hour walk through this lovely park and reflect on my blessings. It's a fine way to begin the day. I listen to the birds sing and watch the sea breeze sway the palm trees and say my prayers. Mostly I thank God for another chance at life. I have a pile of regrets, to be sure, and not being a better father to you and Shannon is at the top of the heap. I can't change what I did. I have changed my life, though. And I hope you'll forgive me for that horrible night, for not being a better father . . . hell, not being a father at all. Please forgive me for all the times I mistreated you, yelled at you for some nonsense (a way to vent my own frustrations), degraded you, called you names. And forgive me for the times I ignored you because I was caught up in the self-involvement of the addict. I am profoundly sorry, son. I pray every day that you'll forgive me, but it took all my courage to write this letter and actually ask you for it. I still don't feel worthy of forgiveness, not entirely. But perhaps you can forgive me anyway. I don't think Shannon can, and won't be able to for many years, and I understand completely.

I also pray we can put the bad memories behind us, wipe the slate clean, and start fresh with a man-to-man relationship. You'll be eighteen in a few months, a man in the eyes of the world, so I sure can't treat you like my little boy anymore. I think about this all the time, scenarios, you know? Us out to dinner talking with honesty and trust and respect—like real friends—about what is going on in our lives, where we are headed.

I have one last thing to ask you. (That's what my counselor keeps telling me, ask for what you want . . . unless it's a drink!) And what I would like from you, Jackson, is a letter. Somehow a letter doesn't seem quite as disembodied as an e-mail or phone call. So I'm hoping you'll write a letter that forgives me. I'll settle for a letter that rips me to shreds, because we both know I deserve it. The hardest thing would be for you to simply ignore me, because then I'll finally realize that you never want to see me again, that there is no chance to salvage our relationship. The very thought pains me. I will have no one but myself to blame, of course . . .

Your mother tells me that Granny Dwyer is taking good care of you and you're doing okay, though not having the season you'd hoped for. I was sorry to hear that, I know how hard you've worked on your game. Keep your chin up, son. I also sensed that your mother is angry with you for leaving the nest before she could boot you out, for refusing to give ammunition against me when her lawyer talked to you, and maybe for looking too much like me. Don't be angry with her, Jackson. As a ballplayer you know that the healing can sometimes hurt more than the injury, and that pain can make you lash out at those trying to help.

The healing is worth the suffering, son. I know that much.

Love,
Jack

I read the letter twice more. I consider tearing it up, and actually rip it a little when I get pissed off thinking back to the night he "hit bottom." In the end I slip the letter into my desk drawer and try to forget about it.

SEVENTEEN

Remember that basketball is a game of
habits. If you make the other guy deviate
from his habits, you've got him.

—Bill Russell,
The Book of Basketball Wisdom

O ur game against St. Joe's starts typically, with the Junior Jagoffs shooting well but not playing much defense, and the result is a five-point lead for the visiting Catholics. St. Joe's has a big man named Leonard who is scoring at will.

Then Chipper Michaels goes down. I can tell by the way he rolled over his ankle it's a bad sprain. A moment later everyone in the gym knows as much because Michaels is not showing a lot of toughness. He's grimacing and beating the floor and crying. His buddies help carry him to the locker room, and I try to look sympathetic.

"Report in, O'Connell," Coach Moran yells, and I strip off my warm-ups and run to the scorer's table. "O'Connell for Michaels," I say, and return to the bench area.

We huddle a minute later, and I nod along with Coach Moran's instructions. Then I almost blow my chance when he says, "Okay guys, let's win this one for the Chipper." My mouth is quivering and about to explode, when Stoner's laugh triggers a general laugh and I'm saved from eternal pinehood.

Coach stares at us, pissed. "Don't see what's so funny about wanting to win a game for your injured teammate," he snaps. "You guys are a bunch of losers." He fumes for a little longer, then looks at me. "O'Connell, Leonard is killing us. You've got to stick some defense on him."

"I will, Coach, " I say, trying to summon the courage to say more. Why not? "Uh, Coach Moran?"

"Yeah, what is it?"

"I was thinking a box and one might work against Leonard."

"With you as the one?"

"Yes, sir. I think I can cover him pretty well, especially with some help on the weak-side."

He mulls it over. If I had been one smidgen less polite, he would have rejected the suggestion out of hand. But what I pitch makes too much sense.

"We're on the same wavelength today, O'Connell," he says. "Except I was thinking a diamond and one myself. Got that? Diamond and one, with O'Connell on Leonard. Everybody get in here. Let's get 'em!"

As we walk onto the court, Stoner strides up alongside me. "Should have said diamond and one, Jackson, then he would have changed it to a box and one, and I wouldn't have to run my ass off up top."

"Sorry, Stoner. I forgot to figure Coach's ego into the equation."

Stoner is almost intense for this game. He went to St. Joe's his freshman year, but was expelled for drug use. All the St. Joe's guys know him, and he thinks, probably correctly, that they look down on him. So he naturally wants to play well and spank them good.

A toot from the ref's whistle and the St. Joe's players jog onto the floor. Leonard eyes me like I'm a pile of horse crap he has to clean up. I saw him play a couple of times last year. He's six-nine and a good natural athlete, but not really dedicated to the game. His mid-range jumper is inconsistent but not so bad you can lay off him. He looks at the ball when he dribbles. Has a couple of effective low-post moves, primarily a very reliable turnaround bank shot from twelve feet on either side of the key.

Mostly, though, he's just bigger than most guys he plays against, and more coordinated than other guys his size. This makes him one of the top centers in the state, although I heard from Thaddeus that he was eaten alive by some really skilled big men at a blue-chip camp last summer.

Just watching Leonard move, I know I'm about three times as quick, and quickness forgives much in basketball, especially size. That's why I made the pitch to coach. It will be fun to get all over the hotshot rather than give him the room he would find in our regular zone coverage.

Leonard plants himself in the low post and I move behind his right shoulder. My left forearm rests lightly on his back and my right arm is extended into the passing lane in the classic post defensive position. He slaps down my arm, I bring it up again, and as he goes to slap it again I dig my elbow into his back as a warning. He turns and glares at me, and the referee blows his whistle and steps between us.

"Easy! I'm stopping this right now. Big man, you can't slap down his arm, that's a foul you do it again. And you," he says, pointing an index finger at my nose, "be mighty careful of that forearm on the back or you're gonna be in foul trouble real quick." I nod and ready myself again.

"Bench jockeys get *so* excited when they finally get in a game," Leonard says with a smirk.

"Leonard, you may think you're the next Kevin Garnett, but personally I think you're the most overrated player I've ever seen in my life."

He turns his head slightly and anger flashes in his eyes. I know he'll try to put me in my place right away with a quick score, and that he'll probably go to his bread-and-butter move, the turnaround jumper. He could nail that four out of five times.

Sure enough, as St. Joe's inbounds, he moves to his spot on the left side of the key and starts calling, "Ball! Ball!" Mindful that the ref under the basket is watching me close, I don't dare muscle him out farther. So he gets the ball on an entry pass with good position. I anticipate that he'll fake to the middle and pivot back the other way for a bank shot. So as soon as he stops his fake—he doesn't really try to sell it, not with a guy six inches shorter covering him—I step quickly to where the pivot will take him and leap.

My hand is on the ball as he releases the shot, a block as clean as a hospital room floor. The ball then falls straight down between us and, shocked at the rejection, he doesn't even move for it. I grab the ball and fire it ahead to Stoner breaking for a lay-up. Even the Jagoffs are pointing at me and smiling and whooping at the play.

Up front, Stoner is actually playing some defense against a guy named Bristow, a stocky but quick point guard. Stoner cuts him off on a drive but slaps his hand on the shot and is whistled for the foul.

As we take our positions for the free throw, Stoner walks by Bristow and says, "Been up on the diving board lately, towel boy?" I don't get it, but Bristow turns crimson and shoots Stoner a murderous look. And then he Shaqs both free throws.

When we have the ball, I sense Leonard watching me very closely. He wants to retaliate by stuffing a few of my shots, but I don't get the ball much. Truth is, I really don't want the ball. I've lost confidence in my outside shot, so I focus on setting good picks, making good passes, boxing out, hitting the boards and playing tough defense. I do have a nice tip-in before the half, and we lead by three.

In the locker room, Moran is full of upbeat talk about our comeback, and even tells me I'm doing a good job. When he goes to take his ritual dump, I walk over and sit next to Stoner. "What's up with the 'towel boy'?"

He smiles. "Well, they have this Olympic-size swimming pool at St. Joe's, and in gym class they make you swim naked . . ."

"What?" I laugh. A few of the Jagoffs laugh as well, and everyone moves closer to Stoner to hear the story. Even Michaels, sulking over on the trainer's table with his foot in an ice bucket, is now smiling and giving Stoner his full attention. For the first time all year, we feel like a team.

"Pretty wild, huh?" Stoner continues. "One of the joys of an all-boys private school. So anyway, at least once a gym period some guy's ladder would extend."

"Oh, dude, I ain't believing this!"

"Swear to god, but really, what's the big deal?" Stoner says, looking harshly at the Jagoffs. "You're a bunch of homophobic jocks, and so were most of the guys at St. Joe's. But tell the truth, who hasn't popped wood for no particular reason? Just happens sometimes, right?"

"Speak for yourself, Stoner," Michaels says. "I need some female inspiration."

More laughter, and Stoner shrugs. "Whatever, Chipper. Point is, the gym teacher would make the guy with the hard-on go out to the end of the diving board and hang a towel over his dick. We called it 'Stiff on the Board.'"

"Stiff on the board," I mumble, "with a towel on the rod." Some more laughter.

"Pretty good, Jax," Stoner says. "Anyway, my buddy Bristow was up there a few times when we were freshmen, so I thought I'd play with his head a little. Seemed to work."

"No doubt," Browner says.

"Cheap psychological ploy," Stoner says. "But the psychology for those guys isn't going to be cheap in the long run. You just know the shrinks are going to be busy with guys who lost their confidence on the diving board at St. Joe's."

We continue to play well in the second half. On defense, I hound Leonard. He shoots over me a few times, but I can see him looking for me, hesitating, wondering if I'm going to block his shot again. And we double-team him whenever he puts the ball on the floor. He tries to pass a couple of times, but Sorenson steals one and the other goes sailing over the head of his cutting teammate and into the stands.

I don't block any more shots, but I steal the ball twice when he tries to dribble around me, and slap it away a couple of times as he brings it up to shoot. He's yelling at his teammates and refs, making angry faces, gesturing in frustration. He reminds me of a spoiled kid, whining because he's no longer getting his way.

We lead by twelve at the start of the fourth quarter. Which is when everything falls apart.

Throughout the third quarter the Jagoffs' defense consisted mostly of yelling, "Miss, towel boy!" whenever any of the St. Joe's players attempted a shot, and this worked very well. St. Joe's also looked lost without their big man controlling the game. Now, though, they have snapped out of their collective daze and are playing some ball. Their passes are crisper, and they aren't trying to force the ball inside to Leonard, who, because of the diamond and one, always has at least two players on him.

Their defense is also more aggressive, except for Leonard, who is still pouting. They close the gap to five points with less than a minute to play.

Coach calls time, and seeing the expression of rage on his face, no one hurries toward the bench. "You let them back in the game!" he shouts. "We had this sewed up, and you weasels let them back in the goddamn game!" Everyone in the stands near us can hear him, including Principal Edwards. Makes me wonder why coaches get away with saying stuff that would get teachers fired.

We stare straight ahead, nodding, except for Stoner, who is kind of smirking. "Dirkson," Moran yells, "you think this is funny? You're the one most responsible for the collapse! Play some damn defense against Bristow, he's killing us!"

"I'm the one mostly responsible for the lead," Stoner counters. "Let's not forget that."

"Don't talk back to me, Dirkson, unless you want to sit out the rest of the game." It's an empty threat and everyone knows it. Moran is a tough guy, and would bench Stoner if he had a capable replacement or if Steve really screwed up, but not for a little backtalk. Stoner mumbles "whatever" and we break the huddle without a definite plan, other than to hustle and play better defense.

St. Joe's does have a plan. Bristow gets a good screen from Leonard on the perimeter and I hesitate to switch because I don't want to leave the big man. Screens are not generally used against zones, but with Stoner alone on Bristow out front, the play works great.

By the time I commit and try to defend Bristow, his three-pointer is away. My momentum carries me into him after he lets it go, and the ref blows the whistle as I knock him down. The ball swishes through the net, and our lead is down to two.

Bristow rises from the floor to take his free throw. We line up, and the taunting begins.

"You're gonna miss, towel boy."

"Was that a towel or a washcloth?"

"All those naked guys turn you on, dude?"

Bristow says, "Mr. Referee, these guys are making rude comments. I think you should assess a technical." We all laugh at his prissy manner, including the ref. Then the ref says, "All of you shut up and play ball."

Prissy or not, Bristow can shoot, and he sinks the free throw. We're up one with thirty seconds left.

Stoner wants to retaliate, I can see it in his eyes, and since he's our leading scorer, who can argue? I set a pick for him on the right side and he launches one of his line drive bank shots as soon as he passes me. This one is just a touch too hard, and Leonard snares the rebound. We hustle back on defense. Leonard is out front again, and once again he moves to set a pick on Stoner. "Right!" I shout, and Stoner, stopped cold by Leonard's bulk, yells, "Switch!" I'm all over Bristow this time, cutting him off as he tries to penetrate. Suddenly he stops and bounces the ball past me. I know where it's going. Leonard has rolled to the hoop and the Jagoffs haven't closed off the middle. I turn and watch Leonard go up for a two-hand dunk, giving them a one-point lead. He pumps his arm and shouts, redeemed from a terrible night.

I glance at the clock. Twelve seconds. The St. Joe's players are excited and forget to press until Stoner has almost reached half-court. He passes over a double-team to Browner. I head for the low post, getting in position for a rebound. Browner dribbles down the sideline. A St. Joe's player comes over to trap him. He starts to panic, then sees me in the post and, against his usual instincts, fires a pass to me.

Back to the basket, I see Leonard looming over my left shoulder, cutting off the baseline. He obviously doesn't realize I'm left-handed. So I take a dribble around him into the lane. He's retreating hard to cut me off, and it will be difficult to muscle a lay-up over him, so I pull up about six feet away with a jump hook. The ball nestles through the net as the buzzer sounds, and it takes me a moment to realize what I've done and break into a smile.

Next thing I know Kelly Armstead is running toward me from the stands as the crowd stands and cheers us. "You won the game, Jackson!" she shouts, and gives me a hug. She feels fantastic in my arms, and I hold onto her for a few seconds. Guess she really does like me, if she's willing to hug me when I'm all sweaty and smelly.

In the locker room, Moran gathers us together and says, "You guys didn't deserve that win, except for O'Connell. Nice game, Jackson, way to take it to them." Stoner claps a few times, my solitary supporter. So much for that team feeling. I make a point of going over to Browner and telling him nice pass. He snorts, shrugs, and turns away. The Jagoff.

A scorekeeper comes around with stat sheets. Stoner led us with twenty-five points. I had eight points, eight rebounds, four assists, three steals and one very sweet block. I'd be more pleased except I know I could have twenty points easy if I'd made half the open shots I was too afraid to take. I just didn't have time to think about the last shot. All through my long hot shower, I think about the upside of not thinking.

EIGHTEEN

*I always say that the most dangerous play in
basketball is the open white man.*

—Chris Rock, as quoted
by Ira Berkow in *Court Vision*

The party after the game is at the Beachside Hotel near Sandy Hook. I'm not into parties, and in no mood for one tonight, despite hitting the big shot. I'm thinking more about taking only five shots all game, and wondering why I'm so scared about what I do so well. Even so, I cave to pressure by Kelly. "Jackson," she says, "you're the hero tonight, you've got to go to the party." So I follow her car to the shore in Granny's brown beast.

The party is rocking when we arrive. As we walk toward the sound of voices and music, Kelly's hand brushes mine, and the next thing I know we're holding hands. And then I blow it. When we walk into the party, a senior named Wilson Branchflower says, "Hey, you two going out?"

Kelly says "yes" and I say "no," and she turns to me with a hurt look as Branchflower laughs. "I mean, I don't know," I say to her quietly. "We haven't talked about it."

"No, we haven't, I just assumed . . . I thought you liked me."

"I do like you. Look, you want to walk on the beach? I can't hear much over the music."

Before we can leave, Marvin Renker tries to get us to help him recruit Gerry. "He lives around here and I found him in the phone book," he says. "I'm hoping he'll come peacefully, but if not I plan to kidnap him." We take a pass but wish him luck on the mission, and then head out to the beach.

The ocean is gently roaring and the air smells of snow and salt. We put up our hoods against the cold and head south down the boardwalk. I'm trying to think of what to say. I don't want to hurt Kelly, but I don't know if I'd like to date her or anything. She's not super pretty, though she has all sorts of great expressions, a nice smile, huge gorgeous eyes, and all those smarts. I can't tell her that I think she's sort of average looking, so I decide on a different approach, one that's mostly true.

"Kelly, I don't get it," I say. "You're going to Princeton, you're already taking college classes, why do you want to go out with me? I don't even know what the hell I'm going to do after graduation."

"You underrate yourself," she says. "And if you hang around me, I'll give you some ideas about what to do with your life. That would be a bonus . . . God, I feel like I have to sell you on the idea of going out with me. This isn't doing much for my womanly pride."

"No, no, you're great, Kelly. I'm just surprised, that's all. I mean, you're going away to college in the fall, and I won't be going with you. And you mentioned you're traveling around Europe this summer, and I can't afford to do that. So it doesn't seem like we have much of a future."

Stopping, she turns to face me. "Why are you so into the future, Jackson? You're always living down the road, thinking about how great things will be when you make the NBA or something."

I feel myself blushing with embarrassment that she could so easily read my dreams. "Well, the NBA isn't looking too good at this point," I admit. "And I don't know what else I want to do."

Kelly smiles shyly and puts her hands on my shoulders. "Why don't you kiss me?" So I do. I put my arms around her and kiss her long and hard and sweetly, and then we hold each other awkwardly, our bulky jackets getting in the way.

"That was nice," she whispers in my ear.

"Yeah, it was," I whisper back.

"So are we going out or not?" she asks with a laugh. "I thought this would be a good time to get a definitive answer."

"I don't like the way I look," I confess, and I'm not sure why I tell her this. I'm immediately embarrassed and wish I could reel the sentence back in like a fish.

Kelly pulls back and looks me in the eye, nodding thoughtfully. "That's why you never go to parties, never go out with anyone?"

"Yeah, mostly."

"And the thing with your family last year?"

"Yeah, that too."

"Jackson, a lot of people have acne . . ."

"Not like mine. I have scars. I don't know why I'm telling you this, but after I look in the mirror in the morning, I don't want to talk to anyone all day."

"You're too sensitive, and besides, I'm not exactly a movie star. About your family, I heard some of the rumors going around about you last year and—"

"I don't want to talk about that," I interrupt, and stride quickly away from her and back toward the hotel. I've blown it, and I just want to get in Granny's car and go home.

"Jackson, wait up, I'm sorry."

"Forget it. I just don't want to talk about that."

"Will you wait?" she says, grabbing my arm.

I turn and look at her. "I don't want to go out with you, Kelly. My life is a mess, I'm a failure at the only thing I care about, and I don't understand why you'd want to be around me. I really am flattered that you like me, but I would screw up your life. Why don't you go to the party and have fun? And please, never ask me about my family again."

"I'm sorry, Jackson, I'm very, very sorry. How many times do I have to say it?"

I begin walking away again, but Kelly catches up. "You walk way too fast, Jackson. I'm sorry if I wrecked your night, coming on to you, and bringing up painful subjects."

I slow down and then stop, take a deep breath. "I'm not mad at you, Kelly," I say. "I was for a minute, but it's not your fault. I just really want to go now, okay?"

Raising her hands in a gesture of helplessness, she stays there as I walk away. A moment later she's beside me again, breathing hard from her short sprint. I can almost hear her fine brain sorting through the data and reaching conclusions. At the parking lot she points and says, "Look, there's Marvin and Gerry."

Marvin and a couple of other football players are escorting Gerry Dwyer into the party. He looks like a reluctant guest.

"Come on, why don't we go say hi to Gerry?" she says, taking my arm again. "He wouldn't want you to go without saying hello."

The party is now spread over five rooms. Gerry has headed to the last one, farthest from the music. He's sipping a Coke, sitting on a bed with his feet crossed. He smiles when we walk in.

"More honors students," he says. "I got talked into dropping by."

"We almost had to throw him in the trunk," Renker says.

"You're the only teacher we'd ever invite," Ivory Lewis adds. She's dressed in a very tight pink sweater and jeans, blond hair swept back to emphasize her perfect features. I heard from Danny that she and Thaddeus are heavy, that's why he hasn't been around The High Court lately. I wonder why she's not watching him play against Middletown tonight.

Gerry says, "Nice game, Jackson. You've got to shoot more, though."

"Yeah, you're right. I'm letting all those games of HORSE against you go to waste."

"No, don't think like that. Those games were fun for themselves, not preparation for anything."

Kelly puts a hand on my shoulder. "Okay, you two, no more basketball talk."

"I won't have anything else to say," I note.

"Not true," she says. "You can talk literature. Let's talk literature."

"Let's not," says Ivory, turning and sipping her beer. The three guys around her laugh on cue, all of them wondering how to impress her, how to get her alone. It's like they're trying desperately not to look desperate, and she all but ignores them.

"True, literature's not a great party topic," Gerry agrees. "But I am having an interesting time trying to teach *Romeo and Juliet* to my three freshmen classes."

"What's interesting about it?" Ivory asks.

"Well, Shakespeare loved puns, sly allusions, and double-entendres, and many of them are a bit racy. Things you don't want to come right out and say to a class of young people, so I'm trying to get them to understand by subtle hints."

"We need an example," Renker says.

"Okay, when Mercutio says, 'My naked weapon is out,' I will quietly suggest that he's referring to more than his sword, then move on."

"Whatcha mean?" asks one of Ivory's admirers.

"Mercutio is talking about his penis," Kelly says.

"Precisely," Gerry says. "But like I said, I can't tell that to a bunch of freshmen. One kid figured it out, though. The proverbial light went on and he said, 'Hey, he's not just talking about his sword, he's talking about . . .' Well, what he said cost him a quarter."

Everyone laughs, and laughs louder when Gerry adds, "I was so proud."

"How are you going to handle the part when Mercutio is making fun of Romeo after the Capulet ball?" Kelly inquires.

"Delicately," Gerry says. "Actually, part of his dialogue is cut from the text we use."

"Bet I know which part," Kelly says. "'O, that she were an open arse, thou a popperin pear!'"

"I get, like, part of it," Renker says. "But what's a popperin pear?"

Kelly explains. Her clinical analysis leaves me and everyone else in silence. Her hand is draped casually over my shoulder, and some of the guys are looking at me sort of weird. Then Ivory says, "You have experience with that, huh?"

Kelly looks over at Ivory with a slight smile. "No, that's more your taste, I'd guess. I just know the play."

"Ladies, ladies, let's get along," Gerry says lightly. I'm proud of Kelly for not taking any crap from the Ivory goddess, who is a putdown predator if I've ever seen one. I can't imagine Ivory ever cutting on Thaddeus, but I would guess she's made some nasty remarks about his friends, including me. I wonder how he's handling that.

A few more students have wandered into the room now, including Branchflower. "Hey, Mr. D, cool of you to come by," he says. "You want to smoke a fat one?"

"No, thanks, Wilson. In fact," he says, setting his Coke on the lamp table, "I should be going." As soon as he's on his feet everyone immediately pleads with him to stay. And Wilson says, "I was just kidding, Gerry. I know you got to be careful, being a teacher and role model and all that."

"I like being a teacher, but the role model part eludes me sometimes," Gerry says, sitting down again. "I wish I could be more honest about who I am and what I think."

"Why can't you be?"

"I'd get in trouble, maybe fired."

"Why?"

"Well, take parent-teacher conferences. If I ever told some parents what I really think, they'd complain to the administration and school board."

"So you mean you weren't telling my mom the truth when you told her I was the best student you've ever had and destined for success, fame, and fortune?" Renker asks.

"No, that was true," Gerry laughs. "Except for the parts about the best student, success, fame, and fortune. Usually I err on the side of discretion. Parents don't want to hear anything negative about their kids."

"You don't know my dad very well," Lenny Cox says. "He'd pay you to hear negative stuff about me."

"There are exceptions, but most parents don't want the real dirt."

A newcomer asks Gerry if he wants a drink, another little challenge, and Gerry sighs at having to repeat himself. I can guess he regrets accepting this invitation. "Hey, I've been to parties before, you know, and I don't want to spoil this one. But Monday I'm a teacher again, and it's not appropriate for a teacher to drink with his students, or smoke fat ones, Branchflower. Sorry to sound stuffy, but we might as well set the boundaries."

"Tell us more about parent-teacher conferences," Kelly says, trying to ease the slight tension that's crept into the room along with a half dozen more students.

"Well, okay, there's a difference between what we teachers say to certain parents and what we really mean," he says. "I'll give you some examples. We say, 'Your son has a real passion for technology.' We mean, 'I don't know if he likes girls, but software gets him curiously aroused.'"

That gets a little laugh, and Gerry continues. "We say, 'Joe has a real passion for the military.' We mean, 'Your kid scares me, and I've notified the authorities.'

"We say, 'I think Brittany has a bright future in cosmetology.' We mean, 'She's a narcissistic twit and I'm going to smash her compact.'"

Flashing a glance at Ivory, I see her mouth open in surprise, then force a covering laugh. The remark could obviously apply to her, as well as a few dozen other girls at Highland. Kelly, meanwhile, is howling, and she can't stop. Around school she's usually very controlled, zoned into her ambitious A-student mode, and it's cool to see this looser side of her personality.

When the laughter dies, Gerry continues. "We say, 'Chad is quite an environmentalist.' We mean, 'He roots through my garbage and is in dire need of a shower.'"

"Hey, he's talking about Nichols!" Branchflower exclaims, referring to a strange, skinny senior.

"No, Wilson, I'm talking about you."

"Ah, Gerry, I shower!"

"True, but I've caught you sifting through my garbage can a few times."

"Just looking for your stash, dude."

"Tell us more about the conferences."

"Okay, let's see . . . We say, 'Lee has the potential to be a pretty fair student.' We mean, 'Shamu has a higher I.Q.'

"We say, 'I've seen from Mary's journals that you have a very interesting family.' We mean, 'I gave her fifty bucks and told her to run away.'"

That one kills me, and Kelly, too, and we hold onto each other to keep from falling down. We applaud when Gerry says he can't think of any more falsehoods he's passed on to parents. People begin drifting out, heading to the other rooms. I'm feeling better, and say sure when Kelly asks if I want to dance.

Several people are dancing on the walkway outside the room, ignoring the cold. We look inside and see it's so crowded that people are dancing on the beds.

"I should warn you," I say as we move into the middle of the outdoor group. "I've unintentionally injured people on the dance floor."

"With your coordination? I don't believe it."

"I jump rope to music, but I don't think it would be cool to bring my rope onto the floor, you know? I'd hurt even more innocent bystanders."

Kelly is my opposite on the dance floor. She's a little awkward on the basketball court, but here she's all rhythm and grace, bouncing to the beat while I focus on not stepping on her shoes. I never know quite what to do with my arms and hands during a fast song. Hold them at my sides and I'm Frankenstein. Swing them and I'm Jackie Chan.

Finally I'm rescued by a slow song. I step toward Kelly, put my arm around her back, and she rests her head on my shoulder. "You're right, you're a lousy dancer," she says and smiles at me, and we kiss again. I don't know how I went from letting her down easy to my current situation, but I have no complaints.

NINETEEN

As a kid, I had a vivid imagination in the
back yard. I was player, coach, announcer,
even timekeeper. And if I missed the last
shot at the buzzer, there was always time
for one more—or ten.

—Jerry West,
The Book of Basketball Wisdom

On Sunday, I go to early Mass with Granny, as usual.
I'm making an effort to live more in the moment,
as Gerry puts it, but it's really tough at Mass, when you
watch the same rituals and sing the same songs week after
week. I also seem to have a gift for daydreaming. Practic-
ing basketball alone, I can dream my way to glory, and I
can do it almost as well sitting in a boring class or, in this

case, church. I also hold regular imaginary conversations with gorgeous imaginary girls.

The only time I remember being shocked out of my daydreams during Mass was when a young visiting priest gave a sermon that was actually funny and thoughtful. Laughter from Granny and the other attentive folks punctured the bubble of my daydream, and soon I was also laughing at the priest's family stories, too. Then he said something I've remembered ever since: "My mother cooked dinner with a great deal of love," he said, "and as a result her meals were the best I've ever eaten. The addition of love to anything remakes it into something new and wonderful."

Gerry liked that when I told him. He doesn't attend Mass himself, despite Granny's concern about the state of his soul. He indirectly quoted the priest in class the next week and gave me a sly wink. We all knew that Gerry was teaching with love long before he presented the concept for our consideration.

The only spiritual exercise I engage in at Mass is prayer. I don't mean the general delivery prayers such as the Our Father and Hail Mary. No, I mean the ones I pray myself kneeling next to Granny at the beginning and end of the service.

Actually, I cheat when I kneel, keeping my butt on the pew instead of upright. This takes pressure off my knees, which are afflicted with large, soft bumps below the caps. Known as Osgood-Shlatter Disease, the lumps first appeared when I was a freshman and, as a doctor put it, had bones growing too fast for my body to keep pace. The lumps hurt for a few weeks, and still become sore if I play too much on outdoor surfaces or run more than five miles at a time.

I whispered a summary of all this to Granny during the first mass we attended together. She'd given me a harsh look when she noticed my sit-back-and-chill prayer posture. Still, my explanation didn't really seem to satisfy her. She's old school, and though she doesn't say so, I get the idea she'd prefer me to pray in pain, like a good Catholic, rather than risk pissing off God with bad form.

Anyway, most of my personal prayers consist of wishing my family and friends well and making a few general requests. The Lord is well aware I could do without anymore zits. I also thank God for the things I do have. Like shooting hoops, praying makes me feel better. It's interesting that a desperate or difficult shot in basketball is called a "prayer." The way I see it, every shot is a prayer, tossed skyward with hope and faith and a favorable spin.

After church, Granny insists I stop by the market to pick up a newspaper so she can read about the game and my heroics. She was full of congratulations, and wants to come to the next game. I've managed to keep her away so far. I tell her she'll be disappointed because I spend most of the time on the bench, and haven't been playing well, at least not as well as I'm capable of playing.

"If I'd played up to my ability yesterday, the game would have been a rout," I say as I'm driving home. "I wouldn't have had to beat them with a prayer."

"Don't knock prayers," she says. "We just said some, and you never know when they'll be answered. What's the Tennyson line? 'More things are wrought by prayer than this world dreams of.'"

"Guess literature is a family hobby, huh?"

Granny smiles in agreement.

At the house I make our usual brunch while she scours the sports section. I know she's found the story when I hear an angry snort. "Newspapers!" she says. "They can't get anything right!"

I come over to look. The story about the game is very short. It says, "Jake O'Donnell hit a lay-up with one second left to give Highland a 1-point victory over visiting St. Joseph, bringing the Highlanders record to 5-5 on the season."

"Amazing they could get both my names wrong," I say. "Not even the freshmen on the *Highland Beacon* manage to mangle someone that badly."

During our meal I can tell Granny has something else on her mind. Most likely she's trying to think of a gentle way of raising the issue of the letter. She was obviously curious. Although I appreciate Granny's gentle ways, I decide to save her the trouble.

"That letter the other day was from my dad," I say. "He's out in California, doing pretty well."

Granny coughs and sets down her tea cup. "I wondered about that," she says. "You know, Jackson, I saw his name on the return address. I was worried about how you'd take hearing from him."

"No big deal," I shrug. "I really don't have anything to do with him anymore, and he's way out west. We've gone our separate ways."

As usual, Granny sees right through me. It's almost as if her thick glasses can X-ray my soul. "Family is important, Jackson. You should make an effort to stay in touch with your father, now that he's contacted you." She takes a dainty sip of her Irish Breakfast. "I must say it's about time," she adds.

"He says he didn't know how to go about it."

"I suppose it could be difficult, after everything he put you through."

I nod, eyes down, and Granny changes the subject. This afternoon she's going over to her friend's house in Rumson, as usual, and I decide to run over to Danny's.

On the way, I can't think about anything but Kelly.

After dancing, we went out to her car and had a world-class make-out session. She let me get to second base, but asked me to stop when I began torturing her bra strap. "This *is* our fist date," she whispered. I returned to kissing her, and felt as if I could have done so all night, until our lips were numb and swollen from excess pleasure. I recall everything—the sweet loving look in her eyes, the silky texture of her hair, the softness of her skin—and I catch myself grinning like an idiot. The people in the passing cars must think I really love to run.

I said goodnight the first time at about midnight, and as I was extracting myself from the back seat of her car, I looked up and saw Gerry striding toward the parking lot, moving fast. Ivory Lewis was right behind him, demanding that he stop, and finally grabbing his hand. Kelly sat up next to me, began to say something, then was quiet when I put my fore-finger to my lips and pointed. We couldn't hear what was said, they began talking quietly, but we saw Gerry shaking his head. Then Ivory tugging his hand, and finally putting her hands on his shoulders and pressing herself against him. At that point Gerry turned away, extracted himself from her grip and said, loud enough for us to hear, "No thanks, good-night." Ivory stood there for a second with her hands on her hips, looking pissed. We ducked down as she turned back to the party, not wanting to get caught spying.

And as long as we were there, we thought we might as well say goodnight a while longer.

I want to talk to Kelly more about what we saw. Two of my friends are now involved one way or another with Ivory Lewis, and it sort of has me worried. Plus, the party. It's cool Gerry came but I wonder if he might get in trouble if word gets back to Edwards, who doesn't like him anyway.

The Larsons aren't home when I arrive at The High Court, so I begin shooting around. I haven't had a chance to shoot around by myself lately, and I miss that. Ever since I was nine, and started playing basketball regularly, I've had a cool fantasy life on the court. This enabled me to play for hours without becoming bored. Some neighbors thought I had incredible discipline to practice as much as I did. I associate discipline with something hard, something that you force yourself to do, and that wasn't my situation at all. I just loved to dream with a ball and hoop.

I didn't know until I was older that my fantasies were not very original. A lot of players dream about schooling their NBA heroes and winning big games with miraculous last-second shots. I have a book with pictures of players shooting at rooftop hoops in New York, barnyard hoops in Iowa, telephone pole hoops in Texas, and fish net hoops in Alaska. They're shooting and dreaming everywhere.

For some reason—probably Kelly again—I can't fall into a hoop daydream this time. My light gloves and tight sweatshirt are throwing my shot off a bit, too. I finally adjust when the Larsons pull into the driveway, cutting over to the parking area.

"One shot, Jackson, feed me for one shot," Mr. Larson says, holding out his hands and advancing in a jog-walk toward me. I pass him the ball and he lets his two-hander fly. I catch the rebound a foot short of the rim.

"Nothing but air," says Danny, who appears from the sidewalk behind the fence. "You've got to practice more, Dad."

"Okay, one more," he begs. This time he hits the rim, and that brings a self-satisfied smile to his mouth.

"Champagne brunch must have been pretty good for you to shoot that bad," Danny comments.

"Wonderful brunch, nice spread down at the hotel."

"Mom and Dad have a date by themselves once a week," Danny explains, sinking a free throw. "I had a couple of cookies for breakfast, and they're drinking champagne."

"Remember, boys, you get married, settle down, you have to keep dating your wife, make time for just the two of you, at least once a week. Too many couples, a kid or two comes along, they forget why they got together in the first place."

I'm nodding vigorously. He could have been describing my parents.

"Came across an interesting bit of basketball trivia," Mr. Larson says, finally sinking a shot. "But first, let me ask you, who are the greatest white players in the history of basketball?"

Danny and I look at each other. I say, "I don't know about just white players, but I think I know who the top ten players of all-time were, from all my reading."

"I'll be the judge of that."

"Okay, at center you have Bill Russell, Wilt Chamberlain, and Kareem Abdul-Jabbar. At forward you have Larry Bird, Julius Erving, Charles Barkley, and Karl Malone. And at guard Oscar Robertson, Jerry West, and Magic Johnson . . . LeBron James, Kevin Garnett, and Kobe might be on the list by the time they hang it up."

"No Shaq?"

"Nah, he's overrated and lacks skills."

"Think you're forgetting a certain Chicago Bull and Washington Wizard," Danny says.

"Nope, Jordan is in a league of his own," I smile.

"Pretty good team," Mr. Larson says. "And you got the two key players, West and Bird. Greatest white players ever, bar none."

"How about Dirk Nowitzki and John Stockton?" Danny asks. "And I've heard you talk about Bill Walton and Doug Collins, Rick Barry . . ."

"Collins and Walton might have been great, except for injuries," Mr. Larson says, dribbling the ball around himself. He handles it better than he shoots it. "Barry wasn't a team guy, kind of selfish, though he got one title. Those other guys, well, good players, don't get me wrong, but just not in the same class as West and Bird. And do you know where those two guys are from?"

Danny looks at me and says, "Jackson, the basketball encyclopedia, probably does."

"Cheylan, West Virginia, and French Lick, Indiana, respectively."

"Right, West was from Cheylan and Bird from French Lick, respectfully. And if you take a ruler and put it on a map, with the left edge on French Lick and line it up with Cheylan, you know where the ruler leads?"

"No clue, " Danny says.

"Right here, right to The High Court," Mr. Larson explains proudly. "You think that's a coincidence? I tell you, the next great white ballplayer is going to come from right here in Shoreview. Who knows, boys, it could be one of you."

With that, he throws up another airball.

TWENTY

To shoot is to dream; to shoot is to love.

—Curry Kirkpatrick,
Sports Illustrated story on Chris Mullin

First day of February, the short month that seems so long. My speech is today. When I pitched Gerry my written proposal for a speech on How to Shoot a Basketball, he wrote back sarcastically, "Way to stretch yourself, Jackson." He gave the go-ahead only because the speech is *supposed* to be about something you know well. That narrowed my choices to How to Shoot a Basketball or How to Pop a Zit.

Going first today is Jeannie Nash. Her speech is on How to Make an Apple Pie. She has a bunch of props on a table that she's busy arranging. Her head is down, looking over her props and notes, and then, when she begins talking in a shaky voice, her eyes focus up toward the back of the room. Jeannie makes it through the introduction, then looks down at the twenty-five pairs of eyes on her, stutters, stops, and falls into tears. She drops her pie tin and apple and heads for the door, with Gerry a few steps behind her.

We look around at each other. A couple of students snigger, though not too critically. We all have to face the same eyes, and it can make you feel a little outnumbered.

The door opens and Gerry pokes his curly head inside. "Kelly, would you step out here for a minute? And bring Jeannie's props? Jackson, why don't you give her a hand with the table. The rest of you work on your own speeches or your research paper proposals, which, you may recall, are due at the end of class. You're in charge, Marvin." The door closes.

"You heard Mr. D, get to work!" Renker orders.

"Get real, Marvin," Branchflower says.

"Hey, young man, you want a one-way ticket to Mr. Edwards's office?" Renker asks. Branchflower smirks back. "Mind your manners in my class or it's Edwards time, and don't confuse that with Miller time."

Out in the hall, Jeannie Nash's eyes are red, but she's no longer crying. We set the table down, and Kelly and I start to return to class. Gerry says, "Hold up a second.

Jeannie, how about the three of us instead of just me? That okay?"

Jeannie looks at me and Kelly. "Yeah, I guess."

"Good. Now take it from the beginning."

And she proceeds to show us how to make an apple pie well enough that I almost drool, and without the fear that led to her exit. We follow Gerry's cue and applaud, and she smiles in relief. "Jeannie, I know you don't believe me, but if you can give a speech to three people, you can give one to three thousand. Don't worry," he adds when the dread look returns to her eyes, "we'll work up slowly. Five people out here for your next speech, then ten, and then you should be ready for the whole class. Deal?"

"Okay, deal," she says, shaking his extended hand. "Thanks, Gerry."

He winks. "That's Mr. Dwyer."

We carry the table inside, Kelly smiling across at me, and Gerry says, "Long as you're up here, why don't you give your speech next, Jackson."

"Have to get my prop," I say, noticing a flutter in my stomach. I fetch my worn outdoor ball from my gym bag, feeling better with it in my hands. I recall what Gerry said about not letting the false fear win. I take a deep breath and begin.

"My speech is about how to shoot a basketball," I say. "This is a basketball." That gets a little chuckle and I feel better. "Now to shoot this accurately at a basket requires five elements: a straight elbow, balance, coordination, follow through, and practice."

I hold the ball at shoulder height. "Most beginning players are not strong enough to get the ball over their heads, so they start their shots here. That's fine. As a player gets stronger, and starts playing against better players who could block his shot, he will raise it up."

"Hallelujah!" Renker shouts.

"Quiet!" Gerry snaps.

"The key is to always keep the elbow straight, no matter how high or low you begin the shot. Watch a great shooter like Kobe Bryant, his elbow is pointed directly at the hoop. Michael Jordan was the same way, and so were Larry Bird, Jerry West, Oscar Robertson, all the great shooters in basketball history. Or I should say, most of them. Professional players are so good they can sometimes bypass the fundamentals. LeBron James, for instance, doesn't keep his elbow straight, and he's an excellent shooter. Likewise, Jordan took a lot of off-balance shots, and I read that Jerry West and Tommy Heinsohn both shot the ball with a low trajectory. Usually, the higher the arc, the better your odds of making the shot."

I pause for a second, because I was going too fast. Take another breath. "The key thing to remember is that great athletes are like great artists. A painter can ignore the rules of composition and color if he understands them, and if he's great."

"Or she," Kelly inserts.

"Shhhh!" Gerry spits.

"Or she," I amend. Then I mention that two basket-balls can fit through the hoop at the same time, since the rim is twice the diameter of the ball. "And more than that for a woman's ball," I say, with a smiling glance at Kelly. "There's more room than you think up there, so shooting accurately is not so hard, if you give the ball a chance."

I pause and consider the irony. The sixth element of shooting is confidence—bordering on arrogance—which I don't have anymore. Without the confidence, you don't give the ball much chance at all. I remember the NBA player at a camp in the Poconos a few summers back who hit about twenty straight from way outside. When he finally missed, he looked accusingly at the little kids near the heavy basket support. "Who moved the hoop?" he demanded.

I get through the rest of the speech, and Kelly leads the applause. I don't sit down for long, though. Marvin is up next, and he bribed me with movie tickets to act as his prop while he gives a speech on How to Tackle a Guy and Give Him a Concussion.

At the end of class, I hand Gerry a paper with my research project pitch: The Aztec Game. I briefly outline the civilization and its sport, but don't mention the game's similarity to modern basketball. Gerry might know, of course. I'm guessing that he'll go for it anyway, even if I'm not stretching myself as much as he'd prefer.

TWENTY-ONE

*Naismith may not have envisioned the
physicality and speed of today's basketball
player. But he was inspired, nevertheless, to
create a game like no other, one where the
movement was vertical, the ball tosser's aim
was always upward, and the challenge was to
break free from the bounds of gravity.*

—Peter C. Bjarkman,
The Biographical History of Basketball

The next day, before practice, Kelly pulls me aside,
gives me a kiss, and then looks up at me in her
half-shy way. "Jackson, the Sno-Ball Dance is this Saturday," she says. "Were you thinking of asking someone?"

"Uh, I didn't know there was a dance."

"Well, now you do."

"Right. So you want to go?"

"You don't sound very enthused."

"I'm not much of a dance guy, especially not with Highland people."

"You seemed to have a good time at the party Friday."

"I did. Especially after the party." This inspires another quick kiss.

"All right then, pick me up at seven on Saturday," she says, walking away. "You'll have a blast, trust me."

The following day, over at The High Court, Angelo mentions that they're playing Red Bank this Saturday at home, and I should come to the game if we're not playing.

"We play Friday," I say. "I'd love to watch you guys, but I kind of have something up Saturday."

"Could have something else up Saturday, you come to our game," Danny says with a laugh.

"Tell me more."

Angelo says, "Debbie has this friend, another sopho-more named Christine, and she wants to meet you. She's seen you play, I guess, thinks you're cute."

"Must be blind," Danny adds.

I think it over while shooting some mid-range jump-ers. I didn't really say I'd take Kelly to the dance. She pretty much asked me. And she knows I'm not into it. Despite recent activities, I still don't think of her as my girlfriend or anything. The average looks bother me, and I sort of worry about what my friends will think of her. I know I'm a hypocrite, my looks aren't going to knock anyone over. So why should I have such a high standard for girls? Still, here's an opportunity I can't pass up.

"I'll be there," I say.

"Cool," Danny says. "Better come early, we're drawing big crowds, being undefeated and featuring the top player in the state."

The rest of the week is spent figuring out how to tell Kelly I'm not taking her to the dance. She brings it up a few times, and I nod along like we're still on. I can't think of a convenient lie. Luck enters the game when Kelly isn't in school Friday. She's one of Highland's champion debaters and the team is in Trenton for the day. I wait until late afternoon, just before I have to leave for our game, and send her an e-mail: "Kelly, I'm really sorry, but I can't take you to the dance tomorrow, some important stuff came up. Talk to you later, Jackson."

I feel cowardly and play cowardly, taking no shots during my few minutes on the court, though I'm open several times.

Afterward I head over to Danny's for the night. I spend the next morning shooting around, the afternoon researching the Aztecs at the library, then head over to the game with the Larsons. The guys were right, they're a hot ticket. Folks are coming from all over to see Thaddeus play and join the bandwagon of a winner. Plus, Red Bank has been playing well, so it could be a decent game.

We sit halfway up the stands. I'm next to Mr. Larson, and he seems to appreciate my enthusiastic company. Marty looks bored, and spends most of the game talking chemistry with a friend and ignoring his father's delight and his brother's heroics. And Mrs. Larson, while proud of Danny, doesn't know the game very well. She gets confused with football and says things like, "Danny needs to try for more touchdowns."

It's a close game. Shoreview leads by one at the half, and the lead goes back and forth during the third quarter. Red Bank is dominating the boards. Danny has his hands full with a guy two inches taller than him and just as strong. And on defense, Red Bank is double-teaming Thaddeus and basically letting Ronnie Seals go uncovered. Ronnie's missed a dozen open shots by the middle of the fourth quarter. I wish I could sub for him. I know I wouldn't be afraid to shoot if I played for Shoreview. It would be different somehow.

With under three minutes left, and Red Bank leading by four, Shoreview's perfect record looks in danger. Then Thaddeus seems to awaken to this fact. He pulls up from twenty feet and buries a jumper.

"Let the Thaddeus Fly show begin!" Mr. Larson shouts. And it does. Fly steals the ball a few seconds later, feeds Angelo, and dunks on a perfect alley-oop return pass from our favorite Italian playmaker. The Red Bank players look shaken, and a guard forces a shot that's way off next time down. Danny, aggressively boxing out his larger opponent, hauls in the rebound. He feeds Angelo, and knowing to stick with a good thing, he flips it over to Thaddeus on the wing. Thaddeus fakes a jumper and drives, and when three players converge on him he shovels a pass to Danny, trailing the play, for an easy lay-up. Mr. Larson is on his feet and clapping so hard I wonder if his hands will shatter.

With twenty seconds left Red Bank's point guard nails a three over Angelo to tie the game and silence the crowd. Angelo takes it up slowly, watching the clock and protecting his dribble, and finds Thaddeus coming off a screen by Ronnie Seals. Ronnie clears the side, leaving Thaddeus to go one-on-one. He takes the ball to he baseline, his favorite spot, and isn't fazed when another Red Bank player rushes over to double him. He rises up effortlessly, leans back like Michael Jordan, and calmly sinks a jumper to win the game.

Mr. Larson is beaming afterward while we wait in the stands. "Mark of a great player, he steps up when it counts," he says. "Thaddeus is going places, no doubt about it."

"So one day you think he'll be on your all-time black team?" I ask to tease him. He laughs, wagging a finger at me.

Freshly showered and in the glow of victory, the Shoreview players exit the locker room one by one. Some little kids are actually waiting to get Fly's autograph. He seems happy to oblige, talking to the kids and leaving them smiling, while beside him, annoyed that the attention is focused elsewhere and fidgeting with impatience, is Ivory Lewis.

Danny, Rachel, Angelo, Debbie, and Christine walk up the stands toward us. Christine is as pretty as advertised,

I'm glad to see. As our eyes meet, she blinks, pauses, turns to Debbie and whispers something, then shakes her head.

"Hey, boys," Mr. Larson says. "They gave you a scare, huh?"

"Thought they had us. I forgot we had Superman on our side," Danny says, nodding toward Thaddeus.

"Whoa, that's a fine-looking Caucasian girlfriend he has," Mr. Larson says.

"Ivory Lewis," I say. "She goes to school with me."

"Ivory? Her name is Ivory? Oh, perfect." Then he breaks into song. *"Ebony and Ivory, they're together in perfect harmony . . ."*

"Will!" Mrs. Larson snaps.

". . . side by side on the sideline . . ."

"Dad, cut it out!" Danny says between clenched teeth, embarrassed.

"Okay, okay, I was out of lyrics anyway. At least lyrics I could sing in front of your mother."

"Oh, you," she laughs, patting him on the shoulder.

Angelo says, "Hey, Jackson, this is my girlfriend Debbie, and this is her friend Christine."

"Nice to meet you," I say, shaking their hands. Christine is not smiling and avoiding my eyes. I wonder if she's shy. A few minutes later we all agree to head over to Sal's for pizza. I get there at the same time as Thaddeus and Ivory.

"Hey, Fly, way to come through in the clutch."

"Thanks, Jax, glad you could make it. You know Ivory."

"Sure, how's it going?"

"Fine, Jackson. Thaddeus, I'll be inside in a minute, I have to ask Jackson about some homework."

"Cool, I got to take a leak anyway."

"More information than I needed," she says with a phony smile.

When he's inside, she turns to me. "I can keep a secret if you can. I told Thaddeus I was visiting my cousin in New York last weekend, so if you don't mention the beach party, I won't mention your little Shoreview sophomore to Kelly."

I'm too stunned for a minute to reply and can feel my face burning. "I wasn't planning to mention the beach party, so don't worry," I finally manage.

"Good, we have a deal then."

I think this must be what they mean by a deal with the devil.

"Kelly's really smart," she adds casually, "but she's a little, I don't know, mediocre-looking, don't you think? But then, maybe you're not that picky."

"Leave Kelly out of it."

"Why not? You seem to be."

She heads inside while I fume. I thought about mentioning Gerry rejecting her, but don't want to bring up the fact that he was at the party. I remember how pissed she looked when he blew her off.

The rest of the gang arrives with the loud laughter of winners. It takes me a second to notice that they are minus Christine. Angelo pulls me aside.

"Jax, I don't know how to tell you this. I'm really sorry, dude, but Christine thought you were someone else."

"What?"

"She saw you guys play a couple of weeks ago, right, and I guess you got a player who looks like Danny?"

"Yeah, Browner does, sort of."

"Well she kind of assumed that Danny and he were related and friends or something, who the hell knows how sophomores think? Anyway, she thought Browner was Danny's Highland friend, not you, so she took off. I'm really sorry."

"That's okay, Angelo, thanks anyway." I'm always magnanimous in defeat, and the regularity of my magnanimity is depressing.

Angelo tells me to forget it, come into Sal's for pizza. But I can envision Ivory having cruel fun with this turn of events, so I say no thanks and roll off in Granny's car.

TWENTY-TWO

You could almost say that a free throw is a metaphor. It represents all those things in life that are more difficult than they appear.

—Dr. Tom Amberry,
World's Greatest Free Throw Shooter

I diot, idiot! Idiot, idiot, idiot, idiot!

These are my thoughts as I drive back to Granny Dwyer's. All I can think about is Kelly, and hope she doesn't hate my guts. What was I thinking? This cool, smart, and—yeah—pretty girl really likes me, and I toss her aside for a sophomore with a case of mistaken identity.

How could I have thought Kelly was plain? Maybe if you didn't know her she could look sort of average. Once you really looked at her, though, really checked out her big eyes and sculpted cheekbones, and got to know her, well . . . she's knockout beautiful.

Granny is waiting for me in the kitchen, a cup of tea on the table in front of her and a stern expression deepening the lines around her mouth.

"I'm hoping that you have a reasonable explanation for your actions today, Jackson."

"Kelly must have called."

"She called several times this morning. She also came over here looking for you. You stayed over at Danny's yesterday and most of today. Was it to avoid her?"

I can feel the blood run out of my face. "Not really," I lied.

"Are you sure about that, Jackson?"

I shrug. "Was she mad?"

"Mad. Disappointed. Hurt. Mostly hurt, Jackson. You promised to take her to the dance tonight, right?"

"Sort of."

"Sort of? She says you did, and based on the way you look now, I believe she's telling the truth."

"Yeah."

"So you promised to take her to the dance, then backed out late yesterday with some silly excuse, is that right?"

I shrug and keep my eyes down, feeling like crap.

"You should feel bad, Jackson. She bought a dress, you know, and was very excited about the evening."

"Jeez, a new dress? Just for a dance?"

"A dance may not mean much to you, but it was important to her. Instead of dancing and having a good time, she sat right at this table and cried her eyes out."

The image kills me. I slump into a chair and look at the clock. Almost eleven.

"Too late to call," Granny says, noticing my glance. "And she doesn't want to hear from you now."

"Maybe I'll e-mail her tonight and call her tomorrow. I'm sorry, Granny. I really like Kelly. I didn't mean to hurt her."

"Well, you did. Now you're going to have to earn her trust all over again," Granny says. She takes a deep breath and looks at me with a little smile, which I don't get, since she's basically bawling me out for being a jerk. "That girl is sweet on you, Jackson. It was wonderful to see. I'd forgotten how hard young girls can fall. I think you can get her back, but it will be a big job. Better get started."

"Yes, ma'am."

"And Jackson? Next time why don't you ask an old lady when you have questions about women."

"I will, Granny, promise."

In my room, I send Kelly an apologetic e-mail confessing everything and describing myself with words that include "inconsiderate," "jerk," and the previously mentioned "idiot." In the morning, I send another before Mass. I spend the afternoon shooting in the driveway, and for once it doesn't make me feel better.

When I don't get an e-mail response by that evening, I go to the kitchen, take a deep breath, brace for impact, and pick up the phone.

"Hi, Mr. Armstead," I say when her father answers. "Is Kelly home?"

"Is this O'Connell?"

"Yes, sir."

"My daughter doesn't want to talk to you, and for the record I don't think you're worthy of her attention."

"Yes, sir. I'm very sorry. That's why I'm calling, to apologize."

"I'll give you points for guts, but she's not interested in hearing it." *Click.*

Terrific. Kelly hates me and her old man thinks I'm unworthy. I'm contemplating banging my head against the wall when Granny walks in.

"Couldn't help but overhear," she says. "You did the right thing, and you shouldn't give up, not on a young woman like that. Did you get your check from your mother yet?"

"No, probably tomorrow. I'm pretty much broke."

"Figured as much, so this afternoon on my way back from Rumson I took the liberty." Magician-like, she pulls a bouquet of flowers from behind her back. They are in a small vase that she sets on the table. "Now you don't want to just go up and hand these to her tomorrow. She'll still be mad, and seeing you she's bound to scold you some, and flowers won't put her off. No, you want to write a nice note, put it in the small envelope I happen to have in my desk, and leave them in a place you're sure she'll get them—or have someone deliver them for you."

"Thanks, Granny."

"You're welcome," she smiles.

The next morning, twenty minutes before the first bell—the earliest I've been to school in years—I tape the flowers and note to her locker. This draws the attention of a giggly group of freshmen girls, and I tell them to get lost. I stand by a row of lockers where I can spot Kelly coming and keep an eye on the gift, in case anyone decides to mess with it.

A few minutes later I catch a glimpse of her face and step behind the lockers. Her back is to me when she spots the flowers and slows down. She reads the note, then crumples it and tosses it in the trash. Keeps the flowers, though, so all hope isn't lost.

I don't see her again until fourth period in Journalism. She's typing away at a computer when I enter.

"Hey, Kelly."

Her eyes leave the screen for just a second. "Your zits are looking good today, O'Connell."

"Ouch."

"Flowers aren't going to get you back in my good graces, not after what you pulled."

"Okay. I wanted to tell you in person how sorry I am. I realized too late how special you are, and I'm really sorry I blew it. I've been blowing a lot of things lately . . ."

That gets her attention and she swivels to face me. "This is about *me*, Jackson, what you did to *me*. It's not about you!"

"I know, Kelly, I was just trying to explain, well, forget it . . . I really regret what I did. On the way back from Shoreview Saturday I had like an epiphany . . ."

"Don't strain your vocabulary, you'll hurt yourself. An epiphany is a sudden intuitive insight that fills you with joy. Are you telling me you took *joy* in discovering that you were a jerk?"

"Well, what do you call a sudden intuitive insight that fills you with pain?"

"Your problem." And she returns her attention to the computer, shutting me out like she closed a door.

I drift through the rest of the day, unable to do much except think of her. She makes a point of sitting as far from me as possible in Gerry's class, and I feel rotten as hell. I'm not sure what else to try. I figure tonight I'll explain the situation to Granny and ask if I should persist or mark it down to experience. Painful experience.

After practice I'm shooting free throws, my daily hundred, and have a string of thirty-seven before I Shaq one. I'm sure it has something to do with Kelly strolling onto the court. The ball bounces her way and she holds it.

"You still hate me?" I ask.

"That's not a boring conversational opening, I'll give you that," she says. "And yeah, I pretty much hate you."

"Only pretty much? Pretty much gives me something to work with. You know, some wiggle room."

She smiles in spite of herself and tosses me the ball. I swish a free throw. She recovers the rebound again and walks toward me at the line.

"How about if you throw the ball into my face from five feet away?" I suggest. "Over and over, until you feel better. And after each pass I'll say, 'Thank you, ma'am, may I have another!'"

"Tempting," she laughs. "But I think I'll settle for covering you. If I push you around and hack you, I think I'll get the rest of the anger out of my system."

"Hack away, Kelly. I deserve it."

"You sure as hell do." She bounces me the ball and steps close, shoves me hard on the shoulder and hip, slaps my forearms reaching for the ball, and then looks me in the eye and smiles. It's a look I've seen before somewhere. I have such a powerful sense of déjà vu that I drop the ball and stand there with my mouth open. Then it hits me: Kelly is the one, the goddess of the court, the one with the quick hands and pretty smile.

The girl of my dreams.

TWENTY-THREE

What I have discovered over the years is that success is rooted not only in confidence and hard work but in joy. Passion produces its own energy.

—Tara VanDerveer with Joan Ryan,
Shooting from the Outside

A few nights later I head over to Kelly's after dinner. Her mom smiles and is nice, but her dad's still pissed off. He doesn't shake hands until Kelly pokes him in the side and tells him I'm okay, despite what she said earlier in the week. We're researching our Honors English project and head to her room to work on the Internet.

I find a couple of items on Aztec basketball, and Kelly fills two pages with notes about the composer Puccini, whose music is playing in the background for inspiration. She gets up to replay a song called "Nessun dorma," which she explains is from some opera he wrote. She's cranked the volume, and as I listen to the soaring notes, and watch her mouth the foreign words, and see a tear roll from one of her closed eyes, I fall forever in love with Kelly Armstead.

After wiping her cheek and looking at me with an embarrassed smile, Kelly checks the time. "Still early," she says. "Want to hit the library?"

"Sure," I agree. "My study habits are really improving hanging around you."

We stop at Highland Park on the way to attack each other in her car, but we're cut short by the cold. We straighten our hair and clothes before entering the public library. It closes at 10 p.m., so we have almost two hours.

I find seven books on the Aztecs that look promising. We sit side by side in comfortable chairs facing a window. The library is on top of a hill, and the lights of the Jersey shore are visible in the distance. We settle quickly into our research.

The Aztec game, I learn, was actually passed down from the Mayans. The game resembled basketball mostly because of the vertical stone rings set on the side walls of the arena, usually about ten feet high, though that varied from arena to arena. Some were set lower, and some were on the playing surface.

Like football, it was a rough game, and the players wore pads to protect themselves from the stone walls, the hard rubber ball, and each other. Didn't always work, though. I found accounts of players bleeding to death and dying of exhaustion, because the games often lasted for days. Like football, most of the points were scored by advancing the ball beyond a line on the opponent's side of the arena.

If a player scored a "hoop," the game ended automatically. This was not easy. The diameter of the stone ring was barely larger than the six-inch ball, and the players couldn't use their hands.

Much of the information I find is contradictory. Some sources say the players could use their knees and elbows to move the ball, for example, while others say they could only use their hips. Likewise, conditions and rules varied from place to place. Some arenas were fifty yards long, some hundreds of yards long. Some games involved six players, some ten or more. One source said the captain of the losing team was beheaded following the match, another said it was the captain of the winning team who was "honored," a human sacrifice to the Sun God at the pinnacle of his glory.

Either way, I wondered how they ever got anyone to be captain, given the occupational hazards. And if it was true that the winning captain got the ax, I think it would have been a little tempting for him to encourage the boys to lose one for the Gipper.

Professionals and nobles played the game, and like modern athletes, they were highly coordinated and skillful with the ball. The games were played to "animate and divert" the people between battles, according to one book. And they held religious significance, with the ball and hoops representing celestial bodies and the arena the universe. Plus, right next door to the arenas were the famous Aztec temples.

I laugh out loud when I come across some less ideal features of the game, and Kelly, looking over, smiles and tells me to hush. This one book says the winning team would round up the spectators after the game to rob them. The fans were all betting heavily, so rich gamblers were the primary targets.

Naturally, as soon as the match ended, all the fans ran for the exits to avoid "paying" for their entertainment . . . no doubt about it, NBA players were lucky to come along after the invention of ticket sales and television revenue. I have a mental image of the Lakers, following a home win, surrounding the front row movie stars at the Staples Center. "Enjoy the game, Jack? Great! . . . Gimme the watch."

I yawn, feeling a little sleepy, but keep reading. Next I find an account of a game by a Spaniard, who seemed to have had some leisure time while old Cortez was busy hunting for gold and plotting to convert or kill the Aztecs. Anyway, as I'm skimming through his description, I read words that slow and then stop me. I sit up and reread the passage. The games, he wrote, were played with "joy and delight" by the participants . . . joy and delight . . . Gazing out the window, I think about that for a long time . . .

I can see him then, a smile on his bronze face, sprinting down the court in the Mexican sunshine, giving and taking punishment, trying a hip shot at the side hoop off a pass from his teammate. Then he scrambles back on defense, trying to cut off the giant on the other team, the one man not playing with joy and delight, the bully trying to kill him and his teammates with a knife, now looking him in the eye and daring him to come closer, threatening to cut her, kill her, kill everyone . . .

Kelly shakes me awake, a worried expression on her face. Several people at nearby tables are staring at me, and a librarian is walking toward us saying we'll have to leave if we can't be quiet. We gather our materials and walk out together while the haunting memories recede from my mind.

TWENTY-FOUR

I've spent years trying to forget many of the painful things that happened to me during my childhood. When a door closes, I try my best to keep it shut.

—Cynthia Cooper, *She Got Game*

In her car, I say, "Sorry if I embarrassed you in there."

"You didn't embarrass me, Jackson, I was just worried," she says. "I'm still worried, but I know you don't like talking about it."

"Yeah, the only people I've told the whole story to are a couple of lawyers and cops and a police psychologist. Even Gerry and Granny haven't heard the whole story, though they know most of it."

"Might help to tell someone who cares about you," she says, squeezing my hand. I squeeze back and think about it. Before I really decide what to do, I hear my voice telling her about the last time I saw my father, the night he brought home his friend Billy, the poet and pug who changed our lives . . .

It's around midnight and I'm asleep when they come in. I wake when the door bangs open. I know what that means, another bad one. He's had three bad ones in the last month, hitting Mom once and pushing her to the floor the other times. When I came to her defense, two weeks earlier, he punched me in the face. Wasn't much of a punch, closer to a heavy push, he was so hammered. Still, my father was swinging at my head, you know? I didn't fight back because I was kind of shocked. I helped my mother up the stairs and ignored him. He called me a coward, said I was afraid to fight, even though I could have decked him with one punch. I mean, he was practically falling over as he challenged me. I was thinking about it, but couldn't do it. He always said I lacked the killer instinct . . .

The neighbors called the cops after they heard him cussing and yelling, but Mom refused to sign a complaint and told the cops and social worker to get lost. She was from the same neighborhood he was, and you just didn't file charges for some weak shoves and punches.

This time I hear him laughing in the front hall, and he's talking to someone. I get up and put some shorts on and tiptoe down the hall, peek around the corner.

The old man and his friend have their arms around each other's shoulders and are swaying and singing some sad Irish song, about a rebel being taken to Australia or something. His friend is at least six-six and his sloping shoulders are much wider than my father's. As I'm taking this in, my father looks up and spots me.

"Jack boy," he slurs, and I think about him always calling me "Jack boy" when I have to help him with some chore around the house. "Get yourself down here, want you to meet a great man."

"Great at drinkin' whiskey," the man says, and Dad laughs as if that's hilarious.

"I have to be up early tomorrow, Dad," I say, knowing my excuse will be ignored and might even set him off. I'm stalling, because I vaguely understand what's coming.

"Get down here."

I say, "Dad, why are you doing this again? You promised Mom the last time you wouldn't do this anymore."

"Dad, why you doin' this?" his friend mocks.

"I said get down here!" my father yells, and I hear movement in my parents' bedroom. I walk over and push open the door. Mom is standing and looking for her robe, her eyes half-shut.

"Mom, go back to bed. Dad's home and he's a little drunk. Go back to bed, I'll help him get set up on the couch."

"Sure?" she asks.

"Yeah, just ignore the noise, you know how he gets."

She sighs bitterly, then crawls back under the covers.

I walk downstairs slowly. The stench of booze and cigarettes almost make me gag.

"Billy, this is my son, Jackson. Good kid sometimes, but weak. Weak like his granddad. No toughness in him."

"What you expect, Jack, raising him out in posh-ville? Sure, we didn't have it as good in the city, did we now?"

He raises his fists in front of his face. They resemble two clubs. He looks at me with sad eyes over scarred knuckles.

"Had to use these to get by," he says. "So did your old man. You've gone soft because you never had to fight out on the streets."

"I've been in fights," I say.

"'I been in fights,'" he mocks. "Not like the fights we had, sonny boy. Not with the hard cases we fought, I'll tell you that."

"Billy here's going to teach you to fight," Dad says. He staggers over to a chair and lights a cigarette. "Gonna teach you to stand up for yourself like a man."

Billy swells up with pride and smiles. I notice that he's missing several teeth on both sides of his mouth.

"I'm a poet, too, you know, not just an ex-pug from Dublin and Brooklyn." He stands straighter and attempts to look soulful. "'Thy will be done, my will be done, thy will, my will, hearts fill and words spill . . .' I wrote that."

"It's pretty good," I say.

"Ah, think flattery might get you out of this, don't you now?"

"I don't want to fight him, Dad," I say, backing up a couple of steps.

"I know you don't want to fight," my father says. "You're a chicken, I raised a chicken, here's to chicken," and he lifts a mock toast in my honor.

I work up the nerve to say, "Dad, you're drunk, and I don't want to fight your drunk friend."

They look at me like I'm crazy rather than just stating the obvious. "You hear that, Jack?" Billy asks. "Your boy called you a drunk, and me as well. Said that to my old man and, oh lordy, I would've had to clear out for good."

"I think that's when you did clear out for good, Billy," Dad says, and the pug points at him and they laugh again. They seem to lose interest in me for a moment and I edge closer to the stairs. "Where you think you're going?" Dad yells suddenly. "You're not going up those stairs until you fight like a man." My father looks ugly. Drinking makes him ugly, old, stupid, and mean.

I take another step toward the stairs and Billy walks over and cuts off my retreat. "Will ya dance a bit, lad?" he asks, and throws a jab that brushes my forehead. It all seems a prank, another of Dad's "misjudgments," as Mom calls them, until I see that big fist heading toward my face.

My fists come up automatically and I'm circling when Mom starts yelling from the top of the stairs. She's coming down the stairs yelling at Dad, I don't remember exactly what she says, and then she walks up to Billy, fearless, and shoves him in the chest, tells him to get the hell out of her house this instant. A mistake. Billy backhands her face and it sounds like a gunshot. She goes sprawling across the floor, out cold. Then Billy looks over at Dad, sneering, and Dad stands up, grabs Mom by the wrists and drags her clear of the hall, like she's some large piece of garbage in the ring at the Friday night fights. That's when I know their marriage is over . . .

The noise wakes Shannon, and she's on the stairs, watching Dad drag Mom across the hall. She runs down and goes by us in a flash toward the kitchen. I figure she'll call 911 or hide until it's over. I'm hoping she or the neighbors will call the cops before Billy beats me to a pulp.

He's circling again and now I'm angry enough to fight. I throw a wild left, but he ducks out of the way and I almost fall down from the momentum. I can't believe I missed such a big target so badly.

"Jack, the boy knows nothing about fighting," Billy says, rolling his fists. "Throws a punch like he's throwing a baseball."

He shuffles close and hits me on the cheek. I try some more punches but just get his forearms, if anything. It's amazing the way this fat old drunk can anticipate and move away from my blows. I guess once you've been a fighter, the instincts die hard . . .

He hits me in the nose and I'm bleeding badly. Then I get lucky. The effort of moving Mom was too much for

Dad, and he pukes on the floor. Billy steps back into the large puddle of vomit, slips down on one knee, and falls over on his side. I'm right on top of him, slugging him over and over in the face. He tries to stand and I hit him on the side of his head, behind his ear. That's probably the punch that shatters my hand, though I don't feel any pain yet. The adrenaline is pumping and I'm punching for all I'm worth.

He manages to stand and I back away, scared again. And that's when Shannon, the avenging angel, comes running into the hall with the butcher knife. She runs to Billy and stabs him in the leg, a deep cut. He looks down as if he can't believe it. No sign of pain, though, either from my punches or the knife wound. Shannon is crying and struggling to press the knife farther into his leg when he yanks it out, staggers, and slaps her. She falls down, and he picks her up with his free hand. His forearm is under her chin and her bare feet dangle off the floor.

"She stabbed me, Jack," he says in awe. "Yer little girl stabbed me."

"Okay, Billy, okay. Let her go and let's get you to a doctor." Seeing blood dripping from Billy's leg onto the tiles, and his daughter held hostage in his arm, seems to halfway sober Dad. His friend ignores him.

"Think you can stab a man without paying a price, because you're a little girl?" he asks. Tears are falling from her chin and mixing with the blood and vomit on the floor.

I walk slowly toward them. "Please let her go," I say. "Please, she was just upset. It's over. She's just a little kid."

"And what of that? Kids are dying in India, in Africa, and here in this land, everywhere, everywhere, kids are dying. What's one more child? Child! Ha! A hell child! And I have to teach the little bitch a lesson."

"Billy, yes, let her go . . ." Dad begins, and his friend whirls on him, screams in his face, barking a stream of curses and threats. He slashes Dad's arm with the knife and kicks him in the groin. Dad falls over, rolling slowly back and forth, moaning until he passes out.

I feel totally helpless to protect my sister. If I rush him, he might kill her before I can get her loose. If I do nothing, he might kill her because the demons are loose in his blood. He looks at me over the top of Shannon's head, and with a slow, almost gentle stroke he cuts her under the chin. A line of blood appears and becomes a dripping stream that covers his forearm. "You like that, little girl, you like that?" he says, and kisses her on the ear.

"Why don't you fight me, like you came to!" I shout. "Come on, fight me!" I call him some ugly names, and grab a standing lamp and start toward him.

He holds the knife out toward me. "Oh, you'll get yours, lad, but put down the fucking lamp or I'm gonna cut her throat." He puts the knife back under her chin and I drop the lamp. And then I know the killing anger. The instinct that my father tried to give me is born right then, and I will kill Billy if I can. I will kill him . . .

I say a quick prayer that Shannon will live through this, and it doesn't occur to me until later how strange it is to pray for one life while being determined to take another. But I guess soldiers do that all the time . . .

Billy's eyes suddenly lose their evil edge. He glances around at the destruction in the hall, and maybe he thinks about his life after this. His arm loosens and Shannon drops to the floor. Keeping an eye on Billy, I run over and grab her. He turns his back on us and drops the knife, and I run Shannon into the kitchen. I take a towel from the stove and wrap it under her chin and tie it on top of her head. Then I call 911, shouting that we need police and an ambulance and giving them our address twice, telling them to hurry. My voice sounds weird to me, higher than usual. I try to slow down but can't.

When I go back to the front hall to check on Mom, I take a knife with me. That's when I see Billy laying on his back in the middle of the hall, the butcher knife in his chest. He's dead. I check Mom and Dad. They're both unconscious but breathing. As I walk around the edge of the front hall, I look at the twisting pattern of blood and vomit on the floor, wondering if it's a sign of some sort, and then I go back to Shannon in the kitchen . . .

Kelly's hand is gently caressing my shoulders and the back of my neck. I have more to say and she senses this and doesn't interrupt.

"I wrote out a statement for the cops and two of them made me go over it again and again verbally, while they asked questions. They weren't mean or anything, in fact they were pretty sympathetic and considerate, helping clean me up and get ice for my hand. But they seemed unsatisfied. They looked at each other when I mentioned that I would have killed Billy if I could have done it without getting Shannon killed.

"Finally one of them said it was the clearest case of self-defense he'd ever seen and I should go ahead and admit I killed Billy, because nothing bad would happen to me. I told them I didn't kill him and repeated that part of the story a few more times. They said my father, mother, and sister were out cold, and that it was inconceivable that Billy stabbed himself in the chest and got the knife in that deep. I disagreed with them and mentioned his strength. They said the knife entered his heart at an upward angle, and who killing himself would do that? If you were going to stab yourself, they said, you'd push it right in, not bring it up from a low angle . . . I told them again that I didn't do it, that I would have told them if I had.

"Next they set me up with a psychologist and I told her the story. She said I might have blanked out. Her scenario was that I took Shannon to the kitchen, tied the towel around her chin, then went back and stabbed Billy but blanked it out of my mind. I said I would have remembered passing out or whatever, but she said losing track of time and memory is not uncommon in violent situations. She sounded so assured that she almost had me buying it. I wondered whether it was possible. Whether I could have done something terrible during a sort of time-out of the mind . . .

"They didn't push it any further, though. The cops acted like they were doing me a big favor by calling it suicide."

"Did your father get charged?"

"They were planning to charge him with a felony or two, but then Mom's lawyer got involved in the talks, and they decided they would have had trouble proving any criminal intent on his part. They knocked the charge down to a misdemeanor and required him to enter a treatment center. He was able to keep his law license and pay Mom support. Her lawyer tried to get a statement from me about what a lousy father Dad was, which was mostly true the last few years. But he was a pretty good father when I was younger, and I was sick of the whole business by then. So I refused. That pissed my Mom off, and we haven't been close since."

"And Shannon was okay?"

"Yeah, thank God. She has a scar but it's not too bad. She was messed up for a while. Started smoking weed and drinking—how's that for irony? Mom got her into counseling, and she's doing really well now."

"Jackson, what you told me is terrible, really terrible. But it's not near as bad as some of the rumors going around about you last year."

"Yeah, I know. One of the cops probably told his wife about the case, and she told someone, and in the retelling the story got distorted. Like that exercise we did in Journalism with Mrs. Ford, remember? The rumor that seemed to become the accepted version was that Billy was raping Shannon and I killed him with a knife. A friend of Mom's told her about that one, and she refused to let Shannon go back to school here."

"I don't blame her."

"Me, neither, but I miss Shannon . . . What really got me was that all the guys I hung around with found one reason or another to end our friendship within a week. Some of them looked scared of me, some flat-out told me their parents didn't want them hanging around someone who killed a person, even if it was self-defense. They still look at me funny. I know explaining what actually happened wouldn't help, so I went my own way. I was pretty solitary for a long time, and I think basketball saved me in a way. You know, I could go shoot by myself and dream up friends and teammates to play with and against. And then I was lucky enough to make some real-life friends in Shoreview last spring, and then you this year."

She smiles and kisses me then, and we hold each other for a long time.

TWENTY-FIVE

*It's not the end of the world when you lose a
game, although sometimes as coaches, we feel
like it. There is more to this game of life
than this game.*

—Lenny Wilkens,
The Book of Basketball Wisdom

Among the benefits of going with Kelly is that I
can almost feel my brain growing. She challenges
some of the things I've taken for granted, such as my
worship of basketball. She calls me a zealot of round-
ball, and after I looked up word, I had to agree
with her. Kelly plays on the girls' team, but it's just one
of her many activities, and no more important to her
than the debate team or astronomy club.

"I like basketball," she says when I ask why she doesn't practice more in the off season, "and I shoot around sometimes. Unlike you, Jackson, I have other interests and passions."

"I have another passion—now," I argue, and pulling her close, she has to agree.

The funny part is, I'm finally playing well. We've had two games since that night at the library, and I've come off the bench to score in double figures both games, along with my usual passing and rebounding. Coach played me more, too, which pissed off the Jagoffs. Early in practice today Michaels gives me a cheap shot—tripping me when he sets a pick. I've been cutting into his minutes mostly, so I think it might be intentional, but let it pass. Then, when he's covering me later, I go backdoor and get a nice pass and dunk on him. As I'm coming down I feel my legs being swept out from under me. I manage to roll to my left and so I hit the court on my side, rather than my back and head.

I hear Moran yelling while I'm feeling my hip and seeing if everything still works. After a few seconds I get up and shove Michaels hard in the chest. I'm about to pop him in the face when the other players separate us.

"You Jagoff piece of crap!" I yell.

He yells a few cusses back at me, then adds, weakly, "Hey, it was an accident."

Everybody sort of laughs because they know he's full of it. Coach gets everyone settled down, and while he doesn't call Michaels a liar, he takes him aside and wags his finger in his face, and then makes him run three bleachers. I think it's pretty cool that he has my back, and surprising considering how much Michaels and the other Jagoffs kiss his butt.

. . .

The next day I'm stiff from the fall, and the guys notice when I sit next to them to watch the Highland girls play at Shoreview. I tell them the story and they agree that Highland has a lot of jagoffs, no offense to me and Ivory, who is sitting with Thaddeus.

Danny admits that he's never been to a girls' game before. "They can't jump and half of them waddle more than run," he observes. "A few can shoot and pass, though. I'll give them that."

Rachel, seated next to him, gets huffy. "Oh, that's big of you. Why don't you spout off some more, Mr. Politically Incorrect? Tell me, you think you're better than those women in the WNBA?"

"Yeah."

"No way," Rachel says. "Not even close."

Rachel and Debbie try to draw Ivory into the conversation. She's sitting with her chin resting on her palms, looking bored. Her body language is practically screaming, "I can't *believe* the crap I have to put up with for this guy!"

She answers their questions with her phony smile. When they ask about modeling, she says, "I try to communicate a feeling about the product. I'm very interested in communication, especially interesting conversation." Then she turns away in total dismissal. Rachel and Debbie look at each other, shrug, and give up trying to be nice to Ivory Lewis.

Angelo and Danny give me grief because I loudly cheer anything Kelly does that is remotely positive, including fouls.

"Good foul," I clap. "Smart play."

"Man, Jackson, you got it bad," Angelo says.

"Figures he'd fall in love with a six-footer," Danny adds. "Hey, Jax, you two planning to breed some power forwards?"

"Cut it out, you guys," Rachel says. "I think it's wonderful that Jackson's found a girlfriend." She's been much sweeter to me since hearing about Kelly. One of those female mysteries I haven't unraveled as of yet.

While looking over at my friends, I see Ivory glance at me. Then she whispers something to Thaddeus. I get the general idea that she didn't break any habits and utter a positive comment. This is confirmed when Thaddeus turns to me and says, "She's tall, Jax, for real . . . kind of flat, though."

I stare at him for a few seconds, wondering why he'd say something like that. He's not a putdown predator, just the opposite—until now. Everyone is watching us, and I say, "Why don't you just shut up, Thaddeus?"

Now he's shocked. I see anger in his face for a second, followed by guilt and regret. And it might have ended there if Ivory had kept her mouth shut.

"He's just expressing an opinion," she says. "No, make that a fact."

"Fine, here are some facts for you, Fly," I say. And I mention a couple of reliable rumors I've heard about her. "Everybody got their facts straight now?" I ask.

Thaddeus is on his feet, shouting at me. I stand up and step toward him. Danny and Angelo jump between us, trying to make peace. "Guys," Danny says, "not cool to talk about each other's girls that way."

"Are you going to let him get away with that?" Ivory demands. "You heard what he called me. Are you going to take that from him?"

Thaddeus glares at me. "Think you can talk about my lady, you zit-faced motherfucker?"

"My zits will go away," I say, "but you'll always be black."

That does it. We would have slugged it out right there, but Danny, Angelo, and some of the men in the stands pull Thaddeus away, protecting the star player. They give me dirty looks and I hear a few nasty comments. I want to yell that it isn't my fault, he started it, but I figure it's best to just leave.

. . .

When Kelly arrives at Granny's later that night, she asks me where I went during the game. "I looked up in the stands and you were gone," she says, squeezing my hand.

I tell her the story and her mouth falls open. "So let me get this straight," she says. "You almost got into a fight over my breasts?"

"They were a factor."

"A small factor, obviously," she jokes, looking down. "I hate to agree with Ivory Lewis about anything, but I'm not exactly a swimwear model. What a silly thing to argue over . . . but thank-you for defending my honor." And she kisses me.

Granny comes in to say goodnight, and she and Kelly agree that it's silly when friends fight. "I hope you don't let this end your friendship," she says.

"That's up to him, I guess. He started it by making rude comments about Kelly."

"Well, your comeback about Ivory might have been overkill," Kelly says. "However true it may be. She's a scary person to have as an enemy, Jackson. No conscience whatsoever."

For the next week I'm still pissed at Thaddeus, but I regret the racial comment. I would apologize if he would apologize for what he said about Kelly. Danny says he refuses to talk about it, or much else.

"Thaddeus just shows up and goes through the motions lately," Danny says. "His half-ass game is better than most guys' best, but it's disappointing. His heart's not in it. He missed a couple of days of school and practice, said he was sick. I don't think Coach believed him . . . I don't know if I believe him."

"Doesn't sound like Fly."

"No, something is going on," Danny agrees. "And I'm sure it has to do with that model who's leading him around by the nose."

Two days later, I am called down to the office from gym class. The secretary says I have an emergency phone call, and my first thought is that something happened to Granny. I take a deep breath as I pick up the receiver.

"Hello?"

"Jackson? It's Danny," he says in a voice I hardly recognize. "Thaddeus, man. Thaddeus hurt himself. He's in the hospital. The recovery room. We're going over this afternoon to visit after school, if you want to meet us."

"Yeah, I'll be there," I say, and Danny hangs up before I can ask him any questions.

Angelo and Danny are in the waiting room when I arrive. They nod at me, both looking much older. "He's out of recovery, and in room 503 upstairs, Jax," Danny says. "We were about to go up."

A doctor is leaving as we approach the room. "Excuse me," he says, taking a hasty step back. Big and tall jocks intimidate people sometimes, even when we don't mean to. And the expression on Angelo's face is the most intimidating thing about us, even if he's a small dude.

"Only, ah, relatives are allowed to visit right now," the doctor says.

"We're his friends," I say.

"And teammates," Danny says.

"Practically brothers, Doc," a voice behind us adds. We turn and see Thaddeus's father, Gregory. "It's okay, they can come in and say hello."

"Fine," the doctor says. Gregory Fly nods and the doctor almost runs down the hall.

We all step into the room. Mr. Fly shakes our hands. He's a really strong guy who is a little under six feet, and I wonder how he produced such a tall and lean son. Before we can say anything, he puts his finger to his lips.

"Boys," he whispers, "thanks for coming, means a lot you being here for Thaddeus. He'd thank ya'll himself but he's still out of it, as you can see."

Thaddeus is asleep, his chest rising and falling gently under the white sheet. His head is facing us, and his mouth is slightly open. He has a pink thing that looks a little like a wristband covering half of his left forearm. Tubes and machines surround him, and an I.V. is dripping into his right arm.

We leave and head to the waiting room down the hall. We drink sodas while Fly's dad sips coffee. Curious as I am, I can't bring myself to ask what happened. I wait until he excuses himself to make a phone call and ask Danny and Angelo.

"Slit his wrist," Danny says, looking me in the eye. "He sat on the tracks of the commuter train for a while, then decided to cut himself instead." Recalling this is too much for him and he has to stop and collect himself.

Angelo tells the rest as I stare at them in disbelief. "He bled a lot and was out cold when a guy found him. Guy called an ambulance. He almost didn't make it. They found a whole bunch of drugs on him, too."

I was silent, trying to absorb this information. Thaddeus Fly, the most talented athlete I know, has tried to off himself. Besides his basketball skills, he's popular, handsome, smart, funny, and has a future of fame and fortune all lined up and waiting for him to arrive. He's the last person I ever thought would self-destruct.

"No one knows why he did it," Danny says. "He's been unconscious all day. The doctor said he'll be all right . . . He'll live, anyway."

Thaddeus's father returns with another cup of coffee. After taking a sip, he says, "I'm angry, boys. I just don't know who to be pissed off at. My son was going places, big places, you all know that. His dream might be over now, done . . . I just pray that it isn't. That he'll get another chance . . . When they said he'd live, I was just grateful, you know? But now I want to punish someone."

We nod sympathetically. I'm wondering if Ivory Lewis played any role in the tragedy—it wouldn't surprise me. As I'm considering this, Mr. Fly confirms my thoughts.

"Think that girlfriend of his is partly to blame. She broke up with him a couple of days ago, and he was brooding about it. I was glad they broke up, never did like her, good riddance, you know? I just didn't think Thaddeus would take it so hard." He sighs, looking off to some distant place. "Maybe there's more to it."

"I didn't know they broke up," Danny says. "He wasn't in school yesterday and he hasn't been talking much about anything lately. If she . . . I have never hit a girl, but if she had something to do with this, I could make an exception."

"Wasn't acting himself," Mr. Fly says, his thoughts elsewhere. "I should have noticed sooner. I know," he says, looking over at me, "that you two almost went at it."

"Almost," I nod. "I'm sorry about that."

He shrugs. "Ballplayer stuff, nothing to apologize for. It's just not like Thaddeus. I'm always telling him he's too soft on the court. He hates to fight. Hates it."

A few minutes later a tall, striking black woman whose eyes are a little unfocused walks into the waiting area holding several bags of burgers. Right behind her are two young girls hauling plastic bags filled with sodas. I'm introduced to Thaddeus's mom and sisters, and they ask us to join them for dinner. We decline the offer, probably the first time any of us ever turned down food. We leave the hospital and head to The High Court.

TWENTY-SIX

*The sad truth is that despite all the innova-
tion, flair, and magic African-Americans
have brought to basketball, racism and self-
delusion still bedevil them. Greatness is a gift
from God, though it isn't always rewarded.*

—Nelson George, *Elevating the Game*

Kelly has to interview a teacher about Highland's closed-campus policy during lunch the following day, so she heads off after we finish eating. She was upset to hear about Thaddeus, even if she doesn't know him. I'm still in denial, and half expect the guys to call and tell me it's all a mistake, a big joke, and he's just fine.

When Kelly leaves I decide to find something to read in the library until fifth period. I'm too distracted for anything remotely heavy, so I browse the magazine racks.

I hear the Jagoffs before I see them.

"You hear about Thaddeus Fly?" Browner says. "Tried to off himself. Turns out he's a druggie and a loser after all."

I told Coach Moran I'd be missing practice yesterday afternoon to visit Thaddeus in the hospital, and he said okay reluctantly. He wanted to know what happened, and I didn't know then, only that it sounded serious. Coach probably told the Jagoffs why I was missing, because they buddy up to him and kiss his butt. And now they've seated themselves at a table near me to do what comes naturally, which is act like complete jagoffs.

"Just a dumb nigger," Michaels says. "Can't even figure out how to kill himself. I mean, talk about stupid."

"Heard he had enough drugs on him to open a store," Browner says. "Guess dealing will be his career, now that his basketball days are over."

I walk to the table, lean over and put my hands down, glaring at them. They try to ignore me as they laugh. "Thaddeus is my friend," I say, "and if you two jagoffs say one more word about him, I'm going to rip you apart."

For a moment they look surprised, but they recover. "Ooooo, guess we should be all shook up, Chipper, getting threatened by Mr. Killer here," Browner says. "Doesn't look like he has his butcher knife on him now, so maybe we can handle him."

More talk seems pointless, so I dive across the table at Browner and take him down. He's not expecting an actual fight, because he's six-five and about two-thirty, the biggest guy in the school. It's been years since he had to fight anyone, and he does a bad job now. I'm on top and doing serious damage to his face with my right hand before Michaels tackles me.

He tags me with a couple of good shots before I scramble loose. He tries to take me down from behind and I elbow him in the face and he collapses on the floor, blood spouting from his nose. I turn back to see Browner is now on his feet. His face is red and cut in a few spots, his eyes wild and deadly. He picks up a heavy wooden chair and starts toward me.

"Drop the chair!" a voice orders. I can't see past Browner but I know the voice—Tim Rowlands, head janitor, a small man with a big voice and presence. Browner is still holding the chair, weighing possibilities. "I said drop the chair!" Tim orders. "Put it down or I'm going to club you!"

Browner glances over his shoulder. I still can't see Tim, but I see his broom handle appear over Browner's head.

"You hit me with that broom, my dad will sue your ass and you're gonna lose your crappy job."

"Very true, but I'll find another job before you're out of the hospital. Now would be a good time to drop the chair, kid, because now, see, I would really enjoy clubbing you."

Browner looks me in the eye and slowly lowers the chair, though he keeps it in front of him as he backs away. He thinks I might go for him again, and he's right.

Edwards, Moran, an assistant principal, and several teachers are in the library seconds later, dispersing the curious crowd and keeping us separated. Over the next two hours Edwards brings the fighters and witnesses into his office one at a time, and I have to endure another lecture about my dwindling graduation prospects. I'm really on his screw-up list now, although he seems to believe that I was provoked into fighting. Apparently, a couple of witnesses overheard the Jagoffs' ugly comments.

In the end he decides to suspend us each for two days, with a recommendation for expulsion if any of us are involved in another fight before the end of the year. The "no tolerance" violence policy calls for a week suspension, but the policy is applied less rigidly to varsity athletes, especially if they have a game coming up.

Before leaving school I find Tim and thank him for stepping in and saving me from getting whacked with a chair. "Glad I was in the area, Jackson," he says, shaking my hand. "Enjoy your vacation."

. . .

After school, Kelly is upset when she sees my wounds. "My parents are going to think I'm dating a guy in a fight club!" She settles down when I explain what happened. I ask if she wants to go visit Thaddeus, and she says no, she'll go next time, that me and him have things to talk about.

He's by himself when I step into his hospital room. Flowers are everywhere, and it takes me a minute to find room for the one I have. He's sitting up in bed, looking tired but okay, and not pissed off or anything.

"Looks like you were mixing it up with somebody," he says. "Those cuts are pretty bad."

"Yeah, long story, I'll tell you when you're ready to go to sleep. I got you some reading material," I add, feeling uncomfortable with the fight topic. I set the plastic bag next to his water bottle. "Got you *My Losing Season* by Pat Conroy. Have you read that yet?"

"No, heard it's pretty good, though."

"Excellent."

"Except for the title. Kind of hits home right now."

"You're having a winning season," I say, "and it's not over."

"Maybe, maybe not. My dad's talking to Coach, hoping to get me back playing by the regional tournament, if I'm recovered. I don't know . . . I violated our no-drug policy all to hell. I let everybody down."

"Nobody feels let down, Thaddeus. We all just want you to get better."

"Thanks, Jax. And thanks for coming . . . Was surprised when my dad told me you were here yesterday."

"Sorry about what I said."

"Me, too."

"It just came out . . ."

He looks sad for a moment. "Always comes down to race, don't it? Even with people who aren't racist."

"I don't know, Fly. You hurt me and I wanted to hurt you back, and I said the first thing that came to mind. I wish I hadn't."

"Guess we go with the biggest difference we see, if we don't have time to think about it."

"Maybe. But the biggest difference is our athletic abilities. What was I supposed to say? My zits will clear up but you'll still be a McDonald's All-American?"

He laughs at that. And then out of the blue he asks if I saw Ivory in school today.

"No, but I didn't make it to English class."

"She hasn't called," he says. "I'm still hung up on her, can't stop thinking about her completely."

"What happened? If you don't mind me asking."

"I was stupid, is what happened. She dumped me a few days ago, and was real cold about it. Like we never talked long-term, being together forever and all that. Just bam, it's over, you're outta here, have a good life."

"Wow."

"You know, we'd been going to a lot of parties. I don't even drink, but she's into the designer drugs, meth, all that, and I went along to impress her. So anyway, I had some of those pills and took a bunch after she dumped me, and I just . . . went down and down and down. And then I went and did what I did."

"Jesus, Thaddeus." I'm tempted to make some unkind remarks about Ivory, but I know he won't appreciate them.

"Saw in the paper you had twelve points the other day," he says, moving on to lighter topics. "Not bad."

"Yeah, coach still isn't playing me as much as I'd like, but I'm playing better. I figured out what I was doing wrong. I'd been playing with fear and anger instead of . . ." I stop when I notice he's fallen asleep. And there's nothing about basketball I need to explain to Thaddeus Fly.

As I'm getting ready to leave, Mr. Larson walks in holding flowers. "He's asleep," I whisper.

He looks at Thaddeus, takes in the bulky bandages covering his lower arm. "He was so beautiful on the court," he whispers to me as his eyes brim with tears. "I'm just praying that he will be again some day."

Later that evening I talk about the visit with Kelly. Since she's the smartest person I know, I ask her to explain how William Larson, that unapologetic racist, can also be the warmest and most generous of men.

TWENTY-SEVEN

*When the referee leaves the confines of the
playing area at the end of the game,
the referee's jurisdiction has ended and the
score has been approved.*

—Official Rules of Basketball

We sense something is off soon after arriving in Honors English. Gerry seems to be moving in slow motion. He mumbles about writing in our journals while he takes attendance. Wonderingly, Kelly and I look at each other.

"Gerry—Mr. Dwyer?" she asks. "Is anything wrong?"

He looks up from his attendance book with a bitter smile that I've never seen on his face before. He coughs and struggles to control his emotions. After a moment he says, "It's probably unprofessional to share with you what happened this morning. But we've had such an open and honest relationship, and you've shared so much about your lives with me through your journals and speeches, that I feel like I should be as forthcoming as you've been."

Renker asks, "You okay, Mr. D?"

The smile again. "Not really, Marvin, but I will be. I'm upset because I've been suspended indefinitely. I'm being investigated for inappropriate actions with a student. I'll be gone at least a week, and might not be back at all if they find cause to fire me."

Everyone is stunned and there is not a sound. Then Marvin shouts, "Edwards *is* a motherfucker!"

Gerry holds up his hands and reprimands Marvin. "I'd make you pay a fine, Marvin, but it seems pointless now," he says, and I notice the cuss jar is not on his desk. "Please don't use that kind of language again, okay?"

"Sorry, Mr. D."

"Well, like I was saying, I'm out of here for a while at least. You'll hear a lot of rumors but don't take them seriously. I can promise you that I didn't do anything unethical."

"This sucks, Mr. Dwyer."

"It blows, Gerry."

"Thank you, I appreciate that," he says. "Anyway, some of you were at the party at the beach I attended. That was bad judgment, I shouldn't have gone. But that's all I did wrong. I'm being accused of other things that are completely untrue. I hope you believe me."

"Hell, yes!"

"You're the best, Mr. D!"

"It wasn't a big deal for you to go to the party, Mr. Dwyer," Wilson Branchflower says. "I mean, you made a point of not smoking or drinking. You didn't do anything wrong!"

"No, Wilson, my presence there was wrong. Teachers are asking for trouble when they socialize with students."

"I dragged you there," Renker says. "Let me tell Edwards it was my fault, it's true!"

"The party isn't the big problem, and that's all I can say."

Kelly looks at me, and I nod. Ivory strikes again. And she is conspicuously absent today.

Gerry says, "I've told you all year that I don't like whiners, so I'm not going to whine to you. Quite often what we think are hardships are really opportunities. At the very least they are opportunities to be strong. So whatever happens, don't worry about me, I'll be fine . . . Okay, that ends my lecture for the day."

There is a knock on the door and he goes over to answer. A pizza delivery man is holding five boxes. Gerry pays him, takes the stack of boxes, and sets the food on his desk. We all stay seated, speechless for the second time.

"Hey, you should always eat at a wake," he says, his smile back in place. "You paid for this by cussing like sailors. He'll be back with the sodas in a minute. Come on, dig in."

He doesn't have to tell us twice. Afterward, Jeannie, Kelly, and I help Gerry clean up. I notice that Jeannie is trying to hold back her tears, and they finally fall when she says goodbye to Gerry. "You were the best teacher I've ever had," she says, giving him a hug.

"Thank you, Jeannie, that's very sweet of you to say, and it does me good to hear it right now."

When she's gone, Kelly says, "Ivory got you suspended and maybe fired, didn't she, Gerry?"

He's startled. "You know?"

"We saw her follow you after the party," I say.

"Oh, I see. Well, I suppose I can tell you two about it, if you promise not to mention it to anyone else."

"We won't," Kelly says.

Gerry sighs. "I should have just stuck to my plan, said hello, had one Coke, and left. Or better yet, not let Marvin persuade me to go. But no, I had to stick around and show off my wit. Pretty stupid. You two had left, and so did some others. Then I noticed Ivory looking at me a certain way, invitingly, you might say. And she's a very attractive young woman. She made an impact, I won't deny that, and she knew it."

"That bitch," Kelly says.

"I knew I had to get the hell out of there, so I started to leave, and she followed me, telling me to stick around. Then she grabbed my hand and tried to pull me close. For a second I was tempted, but I'm not stupid. I want to have a long career as a teacher, and the best way to flush that down the toilet is to fool around with a student. So I told her to get lost. She was pretty angry."

"And now she's taking revenge," Kelly says.

"Looks that way. I'm hoping she'll tell the truth once the investigators start pressing her."

"And that's it?"

"That's enough. Again, don't tell anyone, but I'm outta here either way. Even if Ivory tells the truth and I'm cleared, Edwards made it clear he doesn't want me back, and you never get entirely clear of that kind of rumor. So I'll be moving on."

"Where?"

"I was pondering that very question over lunch," he says. "And I think what I'll do is head over to the outdoor shop later and buy myself a huge backpack and some other gear. I'm going to take off for Europe over the summer, or sooner if they fire me. I've always wanted to see Europe and didn't get it done in college. Anyway, after bumming around for a couple months, I think I'll go to graduate school, work toward a master's and maybe a doctorate in literature . . . I know I'll be excited by this soon, maybe even by tomorrow. Right now I'm in mourning, feeling a little sorry for myself. But I won't indulge in self-pity for long."

"Sounds like a good plan," I say. "But you'll be missed here, Gerry."

"By everyone but Edwards," Kelly says.

"The motherfucker," I add, and get a laugh.

"I can't believe Ivory did this," Kelly says. "First Thaddeus, now you."

"She's just a young woman infatuated with her sexual power," he says.

"Gerry, she's the devil incarnate," Kelly insists.

He changes the subject and we talk for a few more minutes, until it's time for basketball practice.

．．．

I'm getting my gym bag from my locker when I see Ivory Lewis slam her locker and hoist two bulging backpacks. She looks scared as hell when she sees me walking toward her. Maybe it's my expression.

"You touch me and I'll scream!"

"First Thaddeus, now Gerry," I say. "You're on a roll."

Seeing I'm not planning to hit her, she puts down the packs and regains some of her composure. "Look, I didn't make Thaddeus do drugs or attempt suicide. I just broke up with him, big deal."

"Yeah, I heard you handled that with your usual sensitivity and compassion. You should come with a warning label, like cigarettes."

"You have no right to judge me! I've had three death threats from insane Shoreview fans because of what Thaddeus did. I repeat, so you can get it through your thick head, O'Connell, what *he* did!"

"Whatever, it's too late to do anything about that. But you can do the right thing for Gerry."

She takes a deep breath. "Gerry shouldn't have been at that party. I just told Edwards the truth about that."

"Bullshit, he never touched you. You threw yourself at him and got rejected."

She's shocked that I know. I can tell she's thinking about lying some more, but she shrugs. "Maybe I exaggerated a little."

"Exaggerated!"

"Hey, he wanted me, okay? I know he did."

"His momentary bad taste shouldn't get him fired."

"Screw you!"

"Tell the truth, Ivory. Do the right thing for once in your life. I'll give you until tomorrow afternoon."

She sneers. "What, is that some kind of threat?"

"There were witnesses," I say. "If you don't clear Gerry, they will, and you'll be in deep shit. You and your parents could get sued."

"Fine, okay, I'll tell Edwards the truth in the morning. Then I'm outta this school, this town, and away from losers like you!"

She picks up the backpacks and turns away. I think about calling her some names but decide she's not worth the effort.

TWENTY-EIGHT

*From what I'd seen so far, there was no
dunking on the reservation.*

—Kareem Abdul-Jabbar,
A Season on the Reservation

The next day, Gerry's suspension and possible firing is big news. Mrs. Ford agrees to let us cover it for the *Highland Beacon*, though she's obviously concerned. Kelly speaks with Gerry for a half-hour on the phone, trying to get him to agree to an interview, but he politely refuses, saying he got all the whining out of his system yesterday. He also reminds her of the promise not to mention the

Ivory incident specifically to anyone, and naturally not include her in the story.

So we interview students about Gerry, compile a few dozen quotes about his brilliance as a teacher and how this sucks big-time. We mention his attendance at the party as a factor near the beginning of the story. Kelly writes an editorial attacking the decision directly and Edwards by implication, and we even find a few teachers willing to comment for the record about Gerry's creativity and flair in the classroom.

If we left it at that, we might have pulled off a slam dunk. But Kelly, being a fair-minded journalist, thinks we should get the administration's side of the story, and she asks Edwards for an interview. He declines, and the following day Mrs. Ford announces in class that he has forbidden any stories about Gerry's situation.

Kelly is steaming, and so are the rest of us.

"This is blatant censorship, Mrs. Ford," she says. "And you know it."

"It's not my call," she replies. "I agree it's newsworthy and should be covered, and I argued your case for a half-hour. But Mr. Edwards is the boss and he said no. You can complain to the Student Newspaper's Association, maybe some groups who defend the First Amendment. But by the time anything is done, this will be old news."

We have trouble working up the enthusiasm to lay out tomorrow's sanitized paper. After class, Mrs. Ford asks Kelly and I to stay for a few minutes.

"You know, when I worked as a reporter on a paper in Pennsylvania, several of us posed as patients to get inside a hospital notorious for shoddy conditions and unsafe practices. Our reporting led to changes at the hospital that helped patients, and maybe even saved lives. We also won several awards and made national news." She pauses for effect and adds, "A good reporter doesn't let a story go because some obstacles crop up. I'm going to be here at 7 a.m. tomorrow to print up this issue. If an unauthorized version were to be printed prior to that and distributed among the students—without my knowledge or consent, of course—well, I couldn't be held responsible, could I? There would naturally be consequences if something like that were to occur . . ."

"Nothing we can't handle," Kelly says. "I mean, if we were to consider such action. We'll see you tomorrow, Mrs. Ford."

I find Tim Rolands during lunch. "Hey, Tim, looking pretty bad out there, think you could leave the window open for me tonight?"

He sets down his soda and looks at me like I've lost my mind. "Did he get you with that chair the other day, Jackson? It's early spring out there, gorgeous, and besides, it's basketball season! You don't need to sneak into the gym during the season." And then the light goes on. "What's up?"

"You heard about Gerry Dwyer?"

"Yeah, nice guy. That was a shame."

"We wrote stories about him being fired, but Edwards won't let us print them in the paper. He doesn't want any criticism. We want to tell the truth, Tim."

"Sounds like a crusade to me. Okay, boys' bathroom window will be open this evening. You have a way to get into the Journalism room and copy room?"

"Uh, no, we weren't that far along in our planning."

"I'll leave them open, too. Teachers forget to lock their rooms all the time, anyway."

"Thanks, Tim."

"You owe me two now, Jackson. But I'll settle for, say, forty percent of your NBA signing bonus."

"Deal."

. . .

We're back at school at 10 p.m. "So this is what the boys' bathroom looks like," Kelly comments after I help her through the window. "Nothing but urinals."

We saved our stories on disks, so it's a simple matter to lay out the front page again. A few paper jams later, we have the usual 400 copies of the *Highland Beacon* printed up.

Next we take the papers down to the locker pit. This is Kelly's idea, so Edwards can't stop us from distributing them in the morning. We slip an issue in every senior and junior locker and every fourth locker for sophomores and freshmen. Afterwards, we sip sodas and admire our work, relishing the secret mission in the dark and quiet school. It seems sort of like a dream, with the quiet and shadows, and since I'm tired I tell Kelly that I've had some dreams about her. Stuff comes out when you're tired.

She looks a little shocked, so I add, "They weren't dirty dreams or anything. Basketball dreams."

"Figures," she laughs. "I was hoping for sexual fantasies." She says things like that sometimes, with no embarrassment.

"The thing is, I dreamed about you before we got together," I say. "I thought you were pretty in the dream."

"And you don't now!?"

"No, I think you're hot, it's just . . . it was before." I can't tell her that I thought she was pretty in the dream but didn't really notice her good looks in real life until that night at the beach. We talk about dreams for a while, how weird they can be. She hits me with another vocabulary word—*prescient*, which she explains is predicting the future. And she laughs when I tell her about the dream in which I'm falling all over the ice-covered court.

. . .

The following morning I call Gerry and tell him about the switcheroo. He's amused but concerned for us. At school, everyone is talking about the story. Kelly and I are summoned to Edwards's office second period, pretty much like we figured. He's holding a copy of the paper. The front-page headline reads, *Popular Teacher Suspended by Party Pooper.*

"Mrs. Ford came to me this morning and said some-one printed up numerous copies of an issue that was not approved," he says. "I will talk to every student on the *Beacon* staff until I get to the bottom of this."

"No need," Kelly says. "We did it."

He stares hard at her. "You have been an excellent stu-dent, Ms. Armstead, and I don't understand this behavior from you."

"You were wrong to kill the issue," Kelly says. "That was censorship."

"No, that was my prerogative. This is a school paper, and as principal I ultimately have the say over content."

"There've been lawsuits over this issue," Kelly says. "I'm researching them now, but I think you'll find the courts have come down on the side of a free press."

"Let's skip the legal aspects for now," Edwards says. "How did you get into the school?"

We're ready for that one. "I left the window open in the Journalism classroom," I say. "Just slightly, so Mrs. Ford and the janitor wouldn't notice. And we got lucky. The copy room was unlocked."

"Teachers copy materials late so it rarely is," Edwards says, annoyed. "Mr. O'Connell, I am tempted to expel you for your behavior lately. You both realize you'll be pun-ished for this, don't you?"

"Yes, sir," we answer together.

"At least you take responsibility. So, you are both sus-pended for two days, beginning Monday. Next, you are both no longer writers for the school paper, though you will stay in the Journalism class. Your basketball seasons are over, too."

He looks at Kelly. "And you are no longer valedictorian. I will not give that honor to a student who engages in this sort of activity," he says, tossing the newspaper on his desk.

Kelly is stunned and at a rare loss for words. Then a voice behind us says, "Don't you think that punishment is a bit over the top?"

We turn and see Gerry standing in the doorway, one foot casually crossed over the other. He's staring calmly at Edwards, who suddenly looks shocked.

"Mr. Dwyer, you were not invited to this meeting. I'd also appreciate you knocking before entering my office."

"Oh, let's cut the crap," Gerry says. "You're punishing good students because you're angry at me, and they made you look bad. Why don't you take your ego out of the equation and do the right thing?"

Edwards stands and points. "Leave now, Mr. Dwyer. Or I'll call security. You're not supposed to be on campus while your case is being investigated. This is highly inappropriate."

"I came to offer a deal," Gerry says.

"No, my decision is final."

"Too bad, because then you're going to have to put up with me and my subversive ways for years to come. I'm having the teachers' union and a lawyer look into the incident, by the way, and I know I'll be cleared. But you could save yourself a lot of trouble here."

Edwards is curious, we can tell. "Explain, Mr. Dwyer."

"Well, Mr. Edwards, if you give these two fine students a more reasonable punishment, I'll resign, effective the end of the year. That's a promise."

Kelly and I look at each other. We know that Gerry's planning to quit Highland anyway. But Edwards doesn't.

Edwards thinks it over. "What did you have in mind?"

"Two-day suspensions only."

Edwards snorts. "That hardly constitutes a punishment at all. No, basketball and the newspaper are out for them, and Ms. Armstead will not be valedictorian."

"No deal, then," Gerry says.

Kelly says, "I'll accept that my season is over, and so will Jackson—if you let him play tonight."

"Out of the question."

"But it's Senior Night, and he's the only senior on the team. Mine was last week, so I know how special it is. He'll get to play the whole game in front of his friends and family. They are counting on this, and so is Jackson."

"Again, you articulate your points very well, but you are straining my patience."

"The quality of mercy is not strained," Kelly says. Gerry and I stare at each other, not believing we're hearing this. "It drops like gentle rain from heaven. It is blessed twice, from he who gives and he who receives. Mercy becomes a principal better than plaques or plaudits. A man becomes a god, in a way, when he seasons justice with mercy, and that's what I hope you'll do, Mr. Edwards. Show some mercy."

He sighs and looks at us, tapping a pencil. He liked Kelly, the super student, right up until she told him about our late-night editing session, so maybe she has some pull. Still, he hates Gerry and me, so that's two-one against. I'm thinking my season is history.

Edwards stands. "O'Connell, you can play in the game tonight. But that's it," he says, pointing his finger at me, "this is your last game representing Highland High. And if you're in my office again this year, you won't be walking with your class in June."

"Kelly remains valedictorian, too," Gerry says. He sits and props his feet on the principal's desk. "Come on, she's the best student who has been through this school in years. She's valedictorian, or otherwise I'm going to stick around, and I can promise you that we'll have a very interesting time together next year."

Edwards looks incensed, but he's nodding. "Fine, she's valedictorian, and you resign in June. That's it. Now get your feet off my desk and all of you get out of here."

Out of politeness, I say thanks to the principal on my way out. He's angry, and he mumbles something about Senior Night finally getting me off the bench. I turn back, pissed, but before I can say or do anything dumb, Kelly slips her hand in mine and Gerry positions himself between me and the principal. They know I want to flip Edwards out the window by his power tie.

Down in the commons, Gerry invites us to go out to a coffee shop. "Since I'm on paid leave and you're too wound-up to go to class," he winks.

We enjoy rehashing the incident while sipping our beverages. "Great speech, Portia," Gerry says to Kelly.

"Why thank you. I knew there wasn't much chance Edwards ever read *The Merchant of Venice*."

"Pretty good paraphrase."

"It was," I agree. "You know, you should think about going to college."

And she hits me for stealing her line.

TWENTY-NINE

There were times when they knew I was a
burning boy, a dancing, roaring, skipping,
brawling boy—moments of pure empyrean
magic when the demon of sport was born in the
howl of my bloodstream, when my body and
the flow of the game commingled in a wild and
accidental mating and I turned into something
I was never meant to be: an athlete who could
not be stopped, a dreaded and respected games-
man loose and rambling on the court.

—Pat Conroy, *The Lords of Discipline*

Shoreview arrives early for our game and the players shoot around in their street clothes. Gowans and
Moran both frown on fraternization, but they're friends
and go inside to Moran's office to shoot the bull, so we do
the same in the stands.

"Win or lose," Danny says, "we all head to Sal's after
the game. I already told Rachel to meet us there."

"Fine by me," I agree, and Angelo and Thaddeus nod. Thaddeus has been out of the hospital two days. He's lost weight and still looks a little shaky. Danny told me he's ashamed about being suspended from the team for the remainder of the season. He tries to be positive anyway.

"Got some good news today," he says. "Coach at Penn called and said I still have my ride. I'm gonna take it. Coach Johns, he was the only one who visited me in the hospital, though a few others called and sent cards. Before this happened, most of these guys were writing me five letters a week, calling all the time, promising me this and that. But as soon as the words 'drugs' and 'suicide attempt' hit the news, I'm no longer the big man. They disappeared, poof, and sent notices that my scholarship offer was rescinded because of character concerns."

"Nature of the business, I guess," Danny says.

"Tell you what, I'm looking forward to playing those schools the next few years," Thaddeus says. "Payback is fun."

"Congratulations on Penn, Fly," I say.

"Thanks, Jax. Wish I was playing against you guys tonight, but I guess I'll have to leave it up to my supporting cast."

They all laugh at that. Then Angelo says, "Hey, I have some news, too."

"You're gonna play naked, right?" Thaddeus guesses.

"No, that's my news," he says. "I'm serious with Debbie and everything, so I'm giving up revealing myself to the general public."

We're all stunned for a couple seconds, then start laughing.

"That's a huge relief," Thaddeus says. "I thought we were going to have to bail you out of jail one of these days."

Danny puts Angelo in a headlock. "So, if you and Debbie get married in a few years and she pops out Angelo Junior, do you worry that your kid will inherit your tendency for public nudity? Your naked spirit, so to speak?"

The newly mature Angelo, after freeing himself, takes the question seriously. "God, I hope not," he says, then laughs with us. "The American Dream, right? You hope your kid isn't as screwed up as you were."

A good crowd is present for the game because of the Highland-Shoreview rivalry. Many Highland fans who would have showed to watch Thaddeus are here now because it could be a decent game. Shoreview is not the same team without Fly, of course, and have split their two games since losing him.

Chipper Michaels doesn't take it well when Moran tells him I'll be starting in his place because it's Senior Night. "He should come in for me, play more than usual, whatever. But it's my starting spot."

"Bullshit, Michaels," Stoner says. "You don't own it. And he should have been starting over you all season."

Moran tells us to cut it out. It's nice hearing my name called in the player introductions. As I stand with the other starters and listen to the National Anthem, I glance around and reflect on the lessons I've learned.

Shoot when you're open.

Pass when you're not.

High in the stands I spot Gerry and Granny sitting together. I smile when they wave to me.

Celebrate the moment.

Give thanks for all you've got.

Kelly is a few rows behind the bench, and I can hear her strong voice as she sings along with gusto. Edwards, leading by example, is in the front of the scorer's table, standing at attention with his hand over his heart.

Run to the sunshine.

Stand up to any fright.

And at the end of Shoreview's bench, standing tall, I see Thaddeus with a vacant expression on his face. I suppose it must feel strange to be watching the team, rather than playing, for the first time in four years.

And most important of all, play with joy and delight.

My final high school game does not start especially well. I miss my first two shots, although they are right on the rim. The difference is that I'm not concerned and plan to continue shooting when I'm free.

Ronnie Seals is covering me. A few plays later, making me prove myself, he gives me room at the top of the key when I rotate over and take a pass from Stoner. I swish the jumper.

And then it begins: the zone, the peaceful place that is dream-like and intense at the same time. Even an average player in the zone can look like an All-Star for a while, and that's me tonight. I hit three straight jumpers from the corner, and know they are going down the pipe when they leave my hand. I grab a rebound, lead a fast-break, and bounce a pass to Stoner for a lay-up.

"Yeah, Jackson, now you're playing!" he says as we run back on defense. He and Angelo, the best point guards in the conference, are engaged in a classic duel. Angelo is too quick for Stoner and drives past him at will, and Stoner simply shoots his line drive bank shots over Angelo at our end.

We're up ten midway through the second quarter, and Shoreview takes a time-out. Jogging to the bench, I feel the cheers of the home crowd wash over me like a wave.

I'm half-listening to Moran when I feel a wet explosion on the back of my neck. Oh, no! A Mt. St. Helens zit has spontaneously erupted! I reach around, wondering if I splattered any fans, and discover that it's not a zit after all, but the remains of a large spitball. I look around the stands, locate the laughing Finks three rows back, and point to him with a smile. He knows I'll seek vengeance in French II next week.

Back on the court, Stoner feeds me in the low post. I use my standard fake, but Ronnie, having been burned by it dozens of times on The High Court, doesn't bite this time. I'm now facing him and leaning back, protecting the ball. Then I see Browner, anticipating my shot, barreling down the lane for a rebound. I extend my arm around Ronnie and hook a soft pass. Browner's so surprised he fumbles it a bit, but manages to convert the lay-up. He gives me a weird look on the way back up the court. He's missed me twice so far and is obviously trying to freeze me out, and obviously expecting me to return the favor. But I respect the game too much to ignore an opportunity, even if it happens to make a Jagoff look good.

At halftime we're up a dozen and Moran is pumped. "You want these people to remember you, O'Connell, keep playing the way you're playing!" When he departs for his ritual dump, Stoner comes over and says, "I just know you're stoned, Jackson. I've never seen you so loose."

"Nah," I reply, "I get high on the rebound."

Gowans obviously had some unkind words for Ronnie's defense at halftime, because he's all over me in the third quarter, and takes a few cheap shots. I hold my ground and ignore him, and nail my free throws when the ref catches him. Danny switches onto me when Ronnie gets his fourth foul at the outset of the final quarter.

"Take it easy on me," he says, "or you can't come over to my house anymore."

"No way," I say, and taking a pass from Stoner on the wing, drain another jumper. Five more jumpers follow, the last a three-point play because Danny, frustrated, runs me over as I release the shot. I watch it swish from the floor. He helps me up, says sorry, and I smile and hit the free throw.

Danny is overplaying me now, trying to keep me from getting the ball, and leaving himself vulnerable to the back door, the sudden sprint to the basket for a pass and lay-up that is the most beautiful play in basketball. It requires non-verbal communication between passer and cutter, and a pinpoint pass to a player running close to full speed.

I catch Stoner's eye and cut hard for the hoop from the left wing. Angelo is all over him so the pass is a little late in arriving. I'm under the basket, going too fast, and slightly off-balance when I leave my feet. I look for a Jag-off to dump the ball off to. They're covered and so, as I begin to descend, I flip a blind left-handed reverse lay-up over my shoulder, with a lot of English, and on this day of days the prayer is answered.

The crowd erupts. Stoner is wearing an awed smile as I pass him, shaking his head. We lead by twenty with two minutes left, and Moran takes me out to a standing ovation. I look at Kelly, clapping and proud, and mouth the words, "I love you."

"Helluva game, O'Connell," Moran says, extending his hand. I shake, thinking about Gerry not holding a grudge against Ivory Lewis for doing something far worse. And I know Moran wasn't trying to intentionally screw me over, just doing what he thought was best for the team, so we're cool. He says, "Maybe I should have, well . . ." He shrugs, knowing it no longer matters.

After leaving the locker room, I kiss Kelly and explain that I'll meet her over at Sal's in an hour, that I have a few things to do. Walking away, I spot Thaddeus leaning against the wall outside the visitors' locker room where his teammates are undoubtedly getting ripped some more.

"Nice game," he says.

"Thanks, Fly."

"You reminded me a little of myself out there," he says, "if I was having an off night."

"That's the best compliment I've ever been given," I say, totally serious, but he laughs. I tell him I'll see him later and start across the darkened gym. Stoner walks up beside me. "That was a good way to go out, dude," he says.

"Yeah, justice in a way. I've played so badly all year I was due a big game."

"Well thirty-two points, I think you got it."

Our footsteps are the only sound in the gym, and Stoner chuckles. "This is awesome, you know? Holding our gym bags, walking across the empty court after a good game. I feel like a pro, kind of. Don't you?"

"Maybe, but seniors are too cool to talk about that," I laugh. "Good luck next year, Stoner . . . Steve."

"Thanks, Jax, same to you."

I head to the pit and take a pen and paper from my locker. I walk to the corner of the commons, sit at a table, and begin. "Dear Dad," I write, and the rest follows naturally, like the echo of a distant dribble.

The End

John Foley is a high school teacher in the Seattle area. He previously worked as a newspaper reporter in the Chicago suburbs and Alaska, covering sports, cops, features and any other beat that didn't require him to attend sanitary sewer meetings. Following a career change to teaching, he worked in Native Alaska villages for several years, which led to his memoir, *Tundra Teacher*. *Hoops of Steel* is based in part on his experiences as a basketball player. Mr. Foley was second string on the junior varsity at a Division III school, but prefers to simply say that he played college ball.

Look for *Running With the Wind,* the sequel to *Hoops of Steel,* in August of 2007.